ALL the Blue Moons
at the Wallace Hotel

Also by Phoebe Stone:

Go Away, Shelley Boo!
What Night Do the Angels Wander?
When the Wind Bears Go Dancing

ALL the Blue Moons

at the Wallace Hotel

by Phoebe Stone

Little, Brown and Company
BOSTON NEW YORK LONDON

Thank you to Nåkki Goranin and to my sisters, Marcia and Abigail, for their friendship and support. Thank you also to Amy Hsu, Laura Marsh, and Sheila Smallwood at Little, Brown. Thank you to Marian Young. And thank you to the Eisen family (you'll know why!) and to my niece Najat, who was the first child to read this. Thank you, too, to my son, Ethan, who did the "french-fry toss." And special thanks to my husband, David, who had to listen to paragraphs and sentences over and over again, sometimes in the middle of the night.

First Edition

The characters and events portrayed in this book are fictitious. Any similarity to real persons, living or dead, is coincidental and not intended by the author.

Stone, Phoebe.
    All the blue moons at the Wallace Hotel / by Phoebe Stone — 1st ed.
        p. cm.
    Summary: Though very different, events in their lives have made eleven-year-old
Fiona and her younger sister, Wallace, close, so when Wallace disappears, Fiona
risks forgoing the dance audition she has worked so hard to get.
    ISBN 0-316-81645-0
    [1. Sisters — Fiction. 2. Ballet dancing — Fiction. 3. Runaways — Fiction. 4.
Death — Fiction. 5. Fathers — Fiction.] I. Title.
PZ7.S879 A1 2000
[Fic] — dc21   00-035211

10 9 8 7 6 5 4 3 2 1

MV-NY

Printed in the United States of America
The text was set in Berkeley Book, and the display type is Mrsdog.

*For my mother, who listened and encouraged,
and for Maria Modugno, who made it happen.*

CHAPTER 1

My Little sister, Wallace, has been making a cardboard doghouse at school for almost a month. As we get off the school bus and head up our hill, I say, "By the way, Wallace, why are you making a doghouse, when we don't even have a dog?"

"Well," says Wallace, "some of the other kids are making these dioramas with all these shells and rocks and stuff. At least the doghouse has a use."

"Yeah, if you happen to have a dog," I say.

"I'd like to have that doghouse," says our friend Kip, who's walking with us. "I could use it to store all my supplies."

"No," says Wallace, "I want to keep it. It says *Roger* above the door in white letters. I painted it really carefully."

"Why did you paint *Roger* there?" I ask.

"Because that's the name I *would* give my dog, *if* I had a dog," says Wallace.

We are walking up the hill, the three of us. The bus doesn't come up this steep hill. The road is too muddy and full of potholes. I took a picture of this road last spring for a science project at school. I called the project "Erosion, It's All Around Us." I got an A.

The wind blows through the tall pine trees above us and Kip runs ahead, his red scarf billowing and rippling like a sail behind him. He dives behind a tree and then as Wallace and I walk by, Kip leaps out and does a handstand in front of us on the road. Then he jumps back to his feet and picks up a rock and tosses it up, up, up in an arc, aiming at the thin, white daytime moon.

It's fall now and already the sky seems to darken early. I can see the beginnings of a pink sunset starting to form in the sky. When the wind blows, maple leaves twirl and soar and gather together in gusts of wind that sweep across the road ahead of us. Wallace lags at the back, walking really slowly, looking at everything, and Kip always keeps to the front, dodging behind a tree now and then.

As we walk, I look down at my feet. They are not pointed straight ahead, but seem to point slightly outward. That's because I have a good turnout. I'm always working on my ballet. Even though I can't take lessons anymore, I still practice all the time. I still want to be a ballerina when I grow up and you have to start early. You have to shape your bones.

The wind roars through the trees and Wallace screams, "Hurry! I think it's going to storm." She rushes ahead, scrambling up the road, dragging her Huckleberry Hound lunch box.

"No, Wallace, red at night, sailor's delight," shouts Kip. "Look at that sky! That means a great day tomorrow."

This is a very windy hill. Sometimes you might think it's storming here and then you get to the bottom of the hill and the air is still and peaceful and the sun is shining, as if it were a whole different world up here. Sometimes it rains here and not down in town.

Once when it was raining, Wallace and I wore our boots and raincoats to school and when we got off the bus, it was a dry, chilly day. I was embarrassed and wouldn't go out at recess because I didn't want anyone to see my boots and raincoat, so I went to the nurse's office and pretended to have a headache. I looked out the window and saw Wallace standing in the sunshine in her boots and raincoat. She was wearing one of those little, plastic rain hats that fold up and fit in your purse, like you buy from a machine in a train station. All the kids were clustered in a circle around her. I think Wallace was enjoying the attention.

Soon we get to the fork in the road where Kip turns off to get to his trailer. Kip lives there with his father. His parents are divorced and his mother lives in Deerlodge, Montana. She works at an insurance agency and when Kip goes out there he gets to do pretty neat jobs at the agency, like putting letters in envelopes and licking stamps. He gets all kinds of stuff there, too, stuff like a key chain that says *Deerlodge Insurance, Montana's*

Best on it. He also has a blotter that he uses on his desk that says *Home on the Range at Deerlodge Insurance,* with a big buffalo on it that looks just like the one on a buffalo nickel.

Kip does a quick cartwheel and then turns off onto his dirt road, walking backward toward his trailer, talking to us all the way. Kip is good at walking backward. He can run backward, too. He doesn't even have to look around to see where he's going!

"I might come over later," he says. After a while we can't see him anymore, we can just hear him through the trees. "I'll see you later over at the Wallace Hotel," he calls out, and it almost seems to echo.

"Was that an echo?" Wallace says, looking at me hopefully. We are always trying to find a real echo around here. So far we haven't succeeded. Sometimes Kip tries to fake an echo in the woods, but most of the time I can detect his voice. You have to be on your toes with Kip. He's usually up to a lot of tricks.

Wallace and I keep on pushing up the hill, the wind carrying Kip's voice farther and farther away. At the top of the hill, we can still hear him calling to us, but we can't hear what he's saying.

Up here where the land flattens out, the first thing you see is our very large, old apple orchard with rows and rows of leaning, twisted apple trees. And beyond that is our house, which is a great, huge place, all silvery and gray because the paint is old and mostly peeled away. Kip calls our house the Wallace Hotel. When he comes over he says, "Say hey, how's life at the Wallace Hotel?"

It's autumn now and the apple trees are full of small, spotted apples. They are small and spotted because no one sprays or prunes or takes care of any of the trees. The wind is high and warm and Wallace and I run down the orchard rows, crushing fallen apples under our feet, filling the air with the smell of apple cider.

We run and we run until we get to our favorite tree at the back of the orchard. Then I climb high up into its branches and look down. I can see the whole orchard in long rows below me. Some of the trees remind me of little, old dancers leaning this way and that. And some of the trees are dead and have lost their bark and stand in their orchard rows, gray and gnarled. Gray. The same color as some of my mother's statues.

I lean back against the tree, and as I'm talking to Wallace I'm doing a port de bras with my arms. (That's a ballet term.) That is, my arm goes out and then up and then forward. I pretend I'm holding an invisible moon in my arms. When I look over at Wallace, she's sitting there on her favorite branch eating two apples at once, one in each hand. Her face is speckled with shadows from the leaves, and she's frowning. I know what Wallace is thinking. She hates her name and she's trying to think up a new one. We usually sit out here after school and think up new names for Wallace.

"What do you say to Kitty?" I ask, looking over at her.

"No," says Wallace, "I don't like it, because it rhymes with itty and bitty and I wouldn't want anyone to call me Itty Bitty Kitty."

"I didn't think of that one, Wallace," I say, pulling an apple off a branch and taking a bite and then throwing it away.

No one cares about this orchard. It has grapevines that are snarled and climbing all over everything. Wallace tried to make grape jelly last week but she didn't use a cookbook. She mixed grapes and cucumbers together and no one would eat it except for Wallace. She had grape-and-cucumber-jelly sandwiches all week for lunch.

"How about the name Isabelle?" says Wallace, her head dipping among the leaves. "Isabelle Irene Whiteside?"

"Hmm," I say, "I like the last name a lot. Do you want to be called Isabelle Irene or just Isabelle?"

Wallace is named after our mother's great-aunt, Dr. Imogene Wallace, the first doctor in Jamaica, Ohio, where our mother's family is from.

"Oh, Wallace, I think Isabelle Irene might just be the perfect name for you!" I call out, and then I slide down the trunk of the tree and Wallace follows. "Let's go tell Mother about your new name."

Wallace and I run through the orchard again. This time the

wind is behind us. I leap and pirouette and leap. When I spin with the wind, it lifts me along higher and faster. Apple leaves pull off the trees and sail in the sky.

At the edge of the orchard, we go down some broken, marble steps into an overgrown sculpture garden. A lot of my mother's sculptures are here, among all kinds of tangled, sharp rose vines and bushes. Even the little, marble benches are swallowed up by long, soft grass. The sky now is ablaze with pink-and-red clouds, and the orchard behind us is twisted and dark against the sky.

We pass the weathered statue of an angel standing above a little pool as if she were guarding it. I remember when there used to be white water lilies and beautiful goldfish in that pool, their orange scales glowing. Now there is just dark, spongy moss and murky water in there. If you look up close at the angel, you can see tiny pit marks from the wind and weather all over her surface. Sometimes in the winter when it's snowing, I can look out from an upper window of the house and see her leaning over the pool, dredged in swirling, white snow.

Wallace sits down on a little, marble bench and opens her lunch box. She gets out a crumbling grape-and-cucumber-jelly sandwich and sits there swinging her feet. I can tell by just looking at Wallace, the way she's sitting there, whistling and eating her sandwich, that she isn't planning to do any homework tonight.

"You could even call me Belle for short once in a while," says Wallace, opening her thermos and taking a sip. Who knows what concoction is in there. Wallace prepared her own lunch today.

"Belle, in French class," I say, "means 'pretty one.' "

Wallace smiles.

While Wallace is eating her leftover lunch, I follow a little, overgrown path through the bushes, trying not to touch the thorny branches that seem to reach out to snag me. In there, under an arch of vines and sprawling rosebushes, I look down and see that one of my mother's statues has fallen over.

"Wallace," I say, "come here and look at this."

We both stand there and look down. Among the autumn leaves and the long, tangled grass, there is a white marble man lying on his back with raspberry vines growing all across his shoulders and rust stains on his cheeks. He lies there, his marble eyes looking up at the sky. Wallace and I don't say anything at all. We just stand there with the warm autumn wind blowing all around us.

CHAPTER 11

"Isabelle Irene Whiteside," I call out, "beat you to the house!" Now Wallace and I run toward the house through the long-uncut yard, the grass matted and yellow and wild, like Wallace's hair.

"Isabelle Irene Whiteside!" I call out again, and I sail over the ground. I always beat Wallace because I'm older and my legs are longer, but she never stops trying. Never.

The wind sweeps across the front of our great, big, silvery-gray, dilapidated house, making a roaring sound as it gets in under the eaves and behind loose shutters. Most of the upper windows are curtained off or boarded up from the inside, and in the reflections in the glass I can see birds gathering in the darkening sky. I look back and see Wallace racing against the wind, trying with all her might to beat me.

Finally she gets to the currant bush right by the front door and she stops, catching her breath.

"I beat you, Fiona," says Wallace, pulling a handful of currants off the bush. "Maybe you were the first one to the door,

9

but you forgot to touch the doorknob, so *I'm* the declared winner!" Wallace rolls her eyes over at me to check my reaction. Then she looks up at the fiery clouds blowing across the sky. I can tell by the way she's tilting her head that she's already counting them. Wallace is always counting the clouds in the sky and not answering when there's a question about who's the winner.

"Forget it, Wallace," I say, "let's go in the house. It's getting dark." I push open the front door and we sort of fall in with our book bags and lunch boxes.

Now that most of the house is empty, it seems even bigger than it used to. There are rooms and rooms upstairs that are closed up and never used at all. Wallace can't remember when this house was lovely, but I can remember.

The front door opens right into the main hall and Wallace starts hopping up the wide, winding stairs right away. They are kind of broken, with spindles missing here and there. The wallpaper in this hall has white lilies all over it and in one place it is bulging and hanging off the wall. As we climb up, Wallace goes behind the paper and stands there eating currants and taking forever.

"Mom," she shouts, "my new name is Isabelle Irene."

I don't think our mother can hear her. She's in the other part of the house. Our mother never comes up these stairs, anyway. She used to have her studio up here on the other side of the ballroom. But she never carves statues anymore. It's been four years since she's done anything like that.

When we get to the top of the stairs, Wallace makes a turn and runs into the enormous ballroom, calling out, "Isabelle Irene Whiteside!" And I leap after her, doing a grand jeté in the middle of the ballroom. We play a lot of kick ball up here, and once Kip broke a pane of glass when he was showing us how to throw a boomerang properly. No one ever fixed the window.

Even though Wallace can't remember, I can remember when there were parties in this ballroom. My father would hire a jazz band, and we would watch our parents dancing and laughing with friends. My father was a great dancer. He used to swing and dip with my mother. The curtains would blow at the long windows, and the paper lanterns draped around the ceiling would glow in the evening light. Sometimes the jazz band played the song "Blue Moon." It was my father's favorite song, and I used to wait to hear it.

Wallace liked "Blue Moon" too, but she was pretty much a baby then and didn't care about anything. Most of the time she just went around stealing olives out of people's glasses when they were off dancing. I tried to tell her it wasn't polite, but sometimes you can't tell Wallace anything at all.

"Look, Fiona, look! I can do this like you do and I don't even have to practice!" says Wallace, jumping now across the little stage at one end of the room. She's faking a swan leap. Her messy, yellow hair sweeps across her face. She rushes back and forth across the stage with her spindly legs flying out from under her. Then she throws herself down on the floor near the ballet barre and says, "Whew, I'm pooped. That was hard work."

Kip helped me set up that barre so I could practice ballet. My friend Nell teaches me all the steps she learns in ballet class. She gave me a pair of her old toe shoes. I don't know how or where or when, but I want with all my heart to be in a real dance recital someday.

My father used to take me to my ballet classes. When we first started going, I was so little that sometimes I rode on his shoulders way high up in the air. Then I would pat the top of his head as we walked along. My father loved ballet so much. The day I learned to spin without getting dizzy, he was so happy he picked me up and circled around the room with me, singing, "Dance, ballerina, dance."

"Wouldn't this make a great statue!" says Wallace, now throwing her arms up over her head and standing on tiptoes. She tries to look stiff and frozen as if she is made out of marble, but I can see her eyes moving and her arms trembling a little. Wallace wants a statue done of her. She talks about it all the time. It isn't possible though, since our mother won't even go in the studio now, never mind carve anything.

A long time ago, she did carve a statue of me in my ballet

shoes and my tutu. I had to pose for that, and I had to stand really still while she got my pose just right. It was hard.

I remember when my mother finished that statue of me. She was polishing it and making the marble look soft as snow. My father and I had just come home from dance class. I had done so well memorizing steps, my teacher had given me a banana-flavored lollipop. I can remember the bright-yellow color now, and the sweet, vanilla taste. My father said to me as we walked into my mother's studio that day, "From now on, if you like, you can have ballet lessons twice a week. And I'll always take you, Fiona. We'll go together."

I look over at Wallace and she hasn't moved yet. She's standing there stock-still, as if we have been playing freeze tag. Then she suddenly comes back to life again and drops to the floor like a rag doll. She lies there pulling the contents out of her book bag, an old leather one that used to belong to our mother. It has a decal of a curly lamb wearing a bow on the flap and a big buckle that Wallace is always fiddling with.

She pulls two books out of her book bag. One book is called *The Borrowers Afloat.* Wallace has read that book about fifteen times at least. The other book is called *Name That Baby! 501 Name Ideas with Definitions.* It shows a cheerful mother holding a smiling baby on the cover.

If Wallace doesn't watch out, she's going to get herself into trouble with this name business. For instance, one time we went bowling with Nell and her little brother, Kenny. (Kenny was really good that day as long as he got to use the little, red bowling ball with the white swirls on it.) When Wallace and I went up to get our shoes, the man behind the counter looked at Wallace and said, "What's your name?"

And Wallace said, "It's Nancy Reynolds."

The man wrote down "Nancy Reynolds" on a form, and then he gave Wallace her bowling shoes.

"Wallace," I said, as we headed for the bowling lane where Nell and Kenny were waiting for us, "this is a place of business. You could get arrested for lying."

Wallace didn't listen to me at all. She just put on her tiny bowling shoes and proceeded to bowl her usual twenty gutter balls in a row, which, in my opinion, has got to be a world record.

Now Wallace keeps pulling more things out of her book bag, a bunch of messy papers, an eraser in the shape of an elephant, a couple of pencils with teeth marks down the side, and a photograph of Mr. Greenjeans from the *Captain Kangaroo* show. We don't have a TV, so Wallace watches *Captain Kangaroo* at Kip's trailer. Kip mails away for things a lot. He sent in a Wheaties box top and got the picture of Mr. Greenjeans. Wallace picks the photo up and holds it above her head, looking at it. She says, "I think Mr. Greenjeans is a really great farmer."

"Actually, Wallace," I say, opening up my book bag and getting out my homework, "Mr. Greenjeans is not really a farmer. He's an actor."

"Oh, yeah," says Wallace, "then where did he get all those vegetables and that cow and everything?"

Wallace is planning to marry Mr. Greenjeans, which, in my opinion, is completely unreasonable. To start with, how is she even going to meet him?

Wallace looks over at my school papers. "Oh, no," she says, slapping her forehead with her hand, "you're not doing another report on that President Roosevelt, are you? You really are too much interested in all that! I didn't even like that play we did last week. You got to be Eleanor Roosevelt and Kip got to be Franklin Roosevelt and I had to be a stupid reporter asking dumb questions like, 'Do you plan to run for a second term, Mr. President?' "

"Wallace, how could you not be interested in someone who was once the president of the United States, someone who was in a wheelchair and couldn't even walk?"

"Who cares!" says Wallace, getting up and skipping around the room. "He isn't our president anymore. Our president now is named Jack Kennedy."

"John F. Kennedy, Wallace. Jack is what you call him if you're one of his buddies. I don't think you're one of John F. Kennedy's buddies, are you?"

"I could be," says Wallace, skipping all the way across the ballroom floor. "For all you know, I could be getting letters from *Jack* Kennedy every day. In fact, I have a letter right here." She picks up a piece of paper and starts reading. "Dear Wallace, great seeing you last week. Love, Jack."

"Let me see that, Wallace!" I say, running after her.

Wallace picks up and zooms across the ballroom. She throws herself over the little stage at the far end of the room and then flips into a small broom closet and slams the door shut.

"Wallace," I say, "come out and let me see that letter!"

She doesn't answer.

"Okay, Wallace," I say, "if I can read the letter, you can borrow my bedspread with the dogs all over it. For one night." Wallace has been trying to get me to give her my dog bedspread for about two weeks. She tries to get me to trade with her, but she doesn't have anything I want. Last week she offered me a dented hula hoop, a pop-it bead necklace, and a Ginny Doll traveling case.

"Nice try, Wallace," I said then.

Now I hear no sound at all coming from the broom closet.

"Okay, Wallace," I say, "you can borrow the bedspread for two nights." No answer.

"Okay, three nights, Wallace. Three nights."

Now I hear some rumblings coming from the broom closet and then I see the letter being slowly shoved out under the door. I pick it up as it comes sliding out.

"I knew it, Wallace," I say. "This letter is just a mimeographed form from school." It says *Dear Mrs. Hopper,* (the Mrs. Hopper part was filled in with ink) *We hope you will attend the Nokawa Elementary School Open House on October 5.*

I know our mother won't go to that Open House, because our mother never goes anywhere. Four years ago, when I was seven, she used to go to things like that and she used to make angels on horseback with graham crackers and melted marshmallow and lots and lots of chocolate.

CHAPTER III

Outside it is completely dark now and a glowing, silver moon hangs low in the sky and looks as if it is trapped in all the branches of the apple orchard. I go over to the French doors at the back of the ballroom and open them. A chilly autumn wind blows in. These doors are covered with peeling paint and the little balcony looks worn. I can remember my father sitting out there reading the *New York Times*. Everything was clean and crisp then and there was a blue-and-white-checked tablecloth on the little table that fluttered in the breeze. It was spring and the orchard was in bloom. I can remember the smell of apple blossoms and the warm buzzing of spring bees.

I look up at that moon again. Wallace and I are always looking for a blue moon in our sky. Usually the ones we see are fakes. A real blue moon is full and very blue in color, not these grayish ones that Wallace calls blue. When you see a real blue moon, you'll know it.

"Come on, Wallace," I say, "let's go downstairs."

"Yeah," says Wallace, stepping out of the broom closet with a huge smile on her face, "and when do I pick up the bedspread?"

Wallace zigzags out the door and into the hall, dragging her book bag by its long strap like a dog on a leash. She clunks down the stairs, hopping down two steps and then back up one. Down two, up one. Down two, up one. It takes about twice as long to get down the stairs that way.

On the first floor, Wallace zips into the drawing room. It's almost the size of our cafeteria at school and it is completely empty. Then she runs into the dining room beyond and I follow her, skipping quickly through the squares of a big hopscotch board we drew in pink chalk on the floor. This dining room is empty, too, except for a built-in sideboard and a stepladder. It's strange in the winter here, because these rooms seem colder than the outside. The windows frost over, and it's fun to stare up close at the frost designs. It feels like you're lost in a country of ice, like in the fairy tale *The Child of Snow.* I found that book upstairs in one of the old bedrooms and one day last summer I read the whole thing.

In the echoing dining room Wallace starts singing, "My body lies over the ocean. My body lies over the sea. My body lies over the ocean. Oh, bring back my body to me."

"Wallace," I say, "it's *Bonnie*. 'My Bonnie lies over the ocean. My Bonnie lies over the sea.' Not *body*."

"No," says Wallace, "my teacher sings, 'My body lies over the ocean.'"

Wallace and I like to do our talent shows in this dining room because of the echo. It makes your singing voice sound really good. We use the built-in sideboard as a stage, and we get up there and sing. We like to make up our own songs. Wallace's songs usually go on too long and a lot of times I have to pull her off the stage.

Then when Kip is here he usually wants to do his "getting shot and rolling down the stairs" number, so we move to the hallway, where Kip can really cut loose and die, over and over again, rolling and tumbling down the stairs without getting hurt at all. He's worked on that trick for a long time. That's when our mother usually calls out from the back room, "What's going on out there?"

And Wallace and I call back, "Oh, Kip is just dying."

And then our mother says, "Oh, okay."

"Isabelle Irene Whiteside," says Wallace, turning in circles now, as we cross the dining room. She calls it out loudly, so it echoes and sounds very elegant. "Isn't it perfect? We finally thought of the most wonderful name in the world," says Wallace, spinning in her bare feet across the floor. Wallace is barefoot most of the time, even though it's autumn now and getting chilly. I like to wear shoes. I have a pair of red ones, with little, leather straps, but when they get wet they dye my feet red, so they aren't exactly perfect.

We skip across the dining room to the large double doors of what used to be the library. Now it's where we live. It's an enormous room with a very high ceiling and a woodstove that is set in the fireplace. Sections of the room are divided off into bedrooms for each of us. There's kind of a kitchen at the back with a hot plate, a refrigerator, a toaster oven, and a little table where we eat. The real kitchen is at the other end of the house. It has enamel counters and green-and-white-tiled floors. But it's icy cold in there in the winter, and the pipes freeze, so my mother has fixed up this library as a kind of apartment.

I push open the double doors and call out, "Introducing Isabelle Irene Whiteside!" Then Wallace steps through the door, with her tangled, blonde hair and her faded, blue dress with the thin, white collar. That dress used to be mine, but as soon as I'm too big for something, Wallace gets it.

"Close the doors, girls. I just got the fire going," says my mother. Wallace and I go over to sit on the brown velvet fainting couch near the fire. We call it the Eleanor Roosevelt couch, because I saw one like it in the Roosevelts' house when we went to Hyde Park a long time ago.

Today our mother is drinking Earl Grey tea. She has a teapot at her feet near the fire. "Would you like some tea, girls?" she asks. I love Earl Grey tea, and I put about five teaspoons of sugar in it and lots of milk. So does Wallace. She might even put in ten, I don't know.

After a while, my mother looks at Wallace, who's sitting there smiling away, looking like she's about to float up to the ceiling, even though her bare feet are dirty and the hem on her blue dress is coming out. I know she's happy, because finally she is not Wallace anymore. She has become Isabelle Irene Whiteside.

Our mother shakes her head. "You were named after Dr. Imogene Wallace, my great-aunt, who was a wonderful doctor who lived in Jamaica, Ohio. Against great odds, she became Dr. Wallace. She never married. She spent her life curing people, and you are named after her, Wallace."

My mother looks back down at her gardening magazine. She starts reading gardening magazines, little by little, in the fall. Then as winter sets in, she has stacks and stacks of them, and all sorts of plans that she draws in notebooks about rose gardens and tulip patios and winding gardenia walks.

"Wallace," our mother goes on, "did you know the Duke of Windsor, who was meant to be king, gave up being king so he could marry Wallis — Wallis, the Duchess of Windsor?"

Wallace kicks her feet and throws her head down on the

Eleanor Roosevelt couch. Then she just lies there for a long time with her hands over her ears.

Wallace doesn't even like our last name, which is Hopper. Sometimes Kip says to her, "Things could be worse, Wallace. What if your first name was Grass? Then your whole name would be Grass Hopper. Wouldn't that be worse?"

Most of the time I don't mind my name, Fiona. But if I *had* a choice I think I would like to have the kind of name that when you go to buy one of those license plates for your bike with kids' names on them, your name would be right there. It must feel really good to be able to go in and buy one of those and put it on your bike. But I think you have to have the name Cathy or Susan or Jane for that.

There are two Susans in my class at school. I guess it would feel really good to be named Susan also, to be the third Susan in my class.

Then when my teacher said, "Susan?" all three of us would answer, "Yes?"

And then we'd make jokes and laugh about it. But inside, all three of us would feel cozy and important and part of the group.

I look over at Wallace now and see that she's still lying there with her head in the pillow. Wallace doesn't often stay upset very long. Already I can hear her singing into the pillow to herself, "How Much Is That Doggie in the Window?"

All around her, among the tables and bookcases and couches, are my mother's tall marble and soapstone statues. Most of them are polished and finished. A few are only half done. I like the one of the woman leaning down as a small dog rushes past her skirts. But my favorite is one of a father with a little girl riding on his shoulders.

My mother's unfinished statues look kind of strange. I don't exactly know what they look like. I guess to me they look like people disappearing from us and going into a world of stone.

CHAPTER IV

WaLLace and I can hear someone whistling through the orchard in the darkness, and we know Kip is out there. He usually comes over after dinner, after his dad has cooked twice-baked potatoes and cube steaks. They have that every night. They never want to try anything different. Every time I ask, "Hey, Kip, what did you have for dinner?" he always says, "Twice-baked potatoes and cube steaks." Then he smiles and rubs his tummy.

Kip practically lives here. He never knocks at our door when he comes over. He just walks in. Right now Wallace and I can hear him thumping across the dining room.

Just as I suspected, Wallace isn't doing her homework tonight. She's back to reading *Name That Baby!* and lounging on the Eleanor Roosevelt couch, eating a bunch of currants that she picked and brought in earlier.

"What do you say to the name Penelope?" she says, looking over at me.

I'm just cutting out a picture of Franklin Roosevelt from an old *Look* magazine that I found upstairs. I'm cutting him out of

25

a boring picture of some meeting at the White House and I'm gluing him onto a beautiful field of flowers I got from a *National Geographic* magazine. My report is almost done.

"What does the name Penelope mean, Wallace?" I say. "Look it up in your book."

"I did," says Wallace. "It means 'one who weaves wild vines.'"

"Wallace," I say, "you can't go around with a name that means 'one who weaves wild vines.'"

"Why not?" says Wallace. "I like to weave pot holders. I could weave wild vines later, when I get older."

"Wallace, I think I hear Kip," I say.

"Me too," says Wallace. And then the double doors creak open and Kip leans through.

"Say hey! How's life at the Wallace Hotel?" he says. Then he leans farther in and adds, "The hotel brochures came from Seattle! They finally got here!" Like I said, Kip is always mailing away for things. He has a three-ring binder under his arm and a big, yellow envelope in his other hand. He whistles and cruises into our living area, waltzing with an invisible partner around our woodstove and past the big, plastic greenhouse our mother set up at the back. Then he leans through the greenhouse door and shouts to our mother, "The hotel brochures got here!"

Wallace gets up, throws her book down, and says, "Hey, Kip, let me see that. Let me see that, Kip!"

We all push on to the Eleanor Roosevelt couch with Kip in the middle, and he opens the envelope.

"Kip," Wallace says, "this is the best one I've ever seen!" Kip collects all these brochures from hotels all across the country, the Howard Johnson, the Biltmore, the Waldorf-Astoria. He hasn't been to them, but he mails away for brochures. You can name any hotel in the country to Kip and he'll tell you if it's a four-star or a two-star hotel. He can also tell you if it's got valet parking and nice views or not.

"Oh, I love that dining room, and look at that swimming pool. Look at those people swimming. Lucky ducks!" says Wallace.

Kip really wants to own a hotel someday . . . maybe even a lot of hotels. "That's why you always beat us at Monopoly," says Wallace, "because you do research and stuff."

"Look," says Kip, "I even got a letter!"

Wallace hangs over the letter, breathing loudly. She reads, "Dear Mr. Kipton Jones, thank you for your interest in the Seattle Towers Hotel."

Wallace squeals and Kip beams.

"That's the third personal letter I've gotten," says Kip, putting it in his three-ring binder with the other brochures.

Our mother comes out from the greenhouse, holding a small plant in a little box of dirt. It is a tiny lily with drooping leaves.

Most of the plants my mother starts in the greenhouse disappear once they are planted outside. They go down into the long grass and seem to be pulled in by the wild, overgrown yard.

My mother stands by the greenhouse door and looks over at us as if we were very far away. She has part of a smile on her face that looks like a sliver of a moon. Our mother doesn't go out much, just to Ralph's Red and White grocery store on the outskirts of town. Kip's father drives her there in his van that says *The Furnace Doctor* on it and shows a man in a white coat with a stethoscope looking into a furnace. When you ride in Kip's father's van, you have to sit on all kinds of tool kits, and there's always a stray furnace pipe rolling around back there.

"Look at this brochure!" Kip calls out to our mother. "This is the best one I've gotten."

"And a letter came with it!" Wallace says.

My mother smiles again, slightly, and goes back into her greenhouse. We can see her shadowy, blurred figure through the plastic as she leans over a plant with a watering can.

Kip's teacher says Kip is "very industrious" to be only eleven years old and know what he wants to be when he grows up. I know I want to be a ballerina. Wallace is always changing her mind about what she wants to be. Yesterday she told Kip that she wants to be a bellhop when she grows up because she wants to wear one of those red velvet suits and one of those little hats with a tassel on top. But in a few days she'll probably change her mind and tell me she wants to be a zookeeper or something like that.

Kip flips through his book of brochures and moves the new one up to the front.

"Wallace," says Kip, looking at her with a big, happy face, "do you still want to live in Seattle, Washington, when you grow up?"

Kip is the one who told us all about Seattle. He went there once with his uncle and he says people live in houseboats and there are hills everywhere and great beards of hanging moss.

"Yes," says Wallace, "I'd like to live in a little trailer that sits right under one of those trees with the beards of moss hanging down. Then when I woke up in the morning, I'd go out and swing on the beard and sing. Even though I've never been there, I do love Seattle," says Wallace. "That's why I call my shoes 'Seattle shoes.' "

"Those are saddle shoes, Wallace," says Kip, "not Seattle shoes."

"My teacher says they're Seattle shoes," says Wallace.

Wallace has been planning to move to Seattle ever since she heard about those beards of moss. Sometimes she tries to leave for Seattle on her own, when she's mad or upset. She puts our cat, Tuxedo, on a leash, and they start walking, but they only get to the end of our long driveway, where the road starts dropping down the steep hill, and then I see her heading back.

"If things work out the way you want, Wallace, you'll be married to Mr. Greenjeans, working as a bellhop, and living in a trailer in Seattle, Washington," Kip says.

"Yup," says Wallace.

"And if things work out the way I want, I'll be a real ballerina by then, only you guys have to help me get some money so I can take ballet class," I say.

"How much is it, Fiona?" Kip says.

"Nell says her classes cost thirty dollars a month," I say.

"Whew!" says Wallace, wiping her brow and then falling over like they do in cartoons to show astonishment and surprise.

"I guess it's hopeless. How can I ever get thirty dollars a month?" I say.

Kip and Wallace and I have tried before to earn some money, but so far we haven't succeeded. Last summer we set up a lemonade stand down on the main road, but not one car stopped. Not even when Kip got the idea it might attract attention if he leaped up in the air and pretended to get shot at the side of the road just as a car went by. He tried it once, throwing himself into the weeds when a Packard whizzed through. But nothing happened except that Kip landed in a bunch of burdocks and Wallace and I had to spend about two hours pulling all the burrs out of his hair.

Another time Kip had the idea he was going to make a bunch

of money by setting up a bug-and-butterfly zoo. He had all these caterpillars and butterflies in little cages and boxes. He tried to charge Wallace and me ten cents each to get in. But we refused. Later he let us in anyway, and Wallace made a donation of a fuzzy, pink caterpillar she had found in the hollyhocks.

"I could make cookies and sell them!" says Wallace.

"Oh, I don't know, Wallace, the last time you made cookies, you doubled something you shouldn't have and the cookies came out just like leather."

"I like leather," Wallace says. "It's chewy!"

Kip lies back on the Eleanor Roosevelt fainting couch and looks up at the ceiling. He blinks his eyes the way he does when he's thinking. He stirs his hand around on the floor behind the back of the couch.

"Hey, what's this?" he says, pulling up an old newspaper. "How long has this old thing been back here?" He starts reading the headline: "POLICE ARE STILL SEARCHING . . ."

"Hey, where did you get that?" I say, getting up in a flash and grabbing the paper away from Kip. Then I rush over to the woodstove and toss it in. In a second it curls up into a black shell of itself, and disappears into the orange fire.

"Geez, Fiona!" says Kip. "You don't have to hide anything from me. I already know all —"

"No," I say, "it's just that the fire was going out. You have to keep throwing stuff in there."

Wallace looks over at me, her eyes suddenly big and serious and gray.

My mother calls from her bedroom area behind the kitchen. She's already in bed, reading. Usually she reads most of the night and keeps her light on even when she does fall asleep. "Did you say it's getting cold, Fiona? Could you go out to the woodpile and get some wood for the fire when Kip goes home?"

Kip usually likes to stay very late, and when it's time to leave he makes up excuses, like "Oh, I think I'll stay five more minutes till the glue dries in my notebook" or "Oh, I think I'll stay five more minutes in case Wallace decides to make those cookies."

Kip gets up now and puts on his red mittens. He goes out into the yard and brings in a load of wood. Then he packs up his hotel brochures and his notebook and some of the homework he was doing and he heads out into the darkness.

I go out after him to bring in another small load of logs. It's so quiet out here. I can hear Kip crackling sticks as he walks home on the little shortcut he made through the woods. Kip has a Davy Crockett flashlight that keeps getting dim and then going out. He has to shake it to get it going, and I can even hear the batteries rattling as he shakes the flashlight.

The sky above is a big, black dome poked with millions of tiny lights. It's such a huge world. In all this hugeness is there a way I can be in a real ballet recital with a real audience? I don't think so. I'll just have to keep working on my own with Nell's help. Nell knows I'm good. She says I have great elevation. But what good does it do to be good when no one else knows or cares?

I'm not going to quit, though, because I keep seeing my father with his arms outstretched, waiting for me after ballet class. I'm running toward him, running to fall into my father's arms. Every time I do a grand jeté. Every time I spin around and around, I'm spinning toward him, around and around and around.

CHAPTER V

When I go into Wallace's room this morning, she's still in bed. It usually takes about ten years to get her up. "Wallace," I say, "come on, we're going to be late for school."

Wallace rolls over and knocks a teddy bear onto the floor. Then she kicks at her covers, and Huckleberry Hound comes rolling out and drops on the rug, too. He's kind of a dumb-looking cartoon dog, but he's Wallace's favorite. He matches her Huckleberry Hound lunch box. My lunch box is from *The Mickey Mouse Club* . . . the "Talent Round-Up." It features all the Mouseketeers in cowboy and cowgirl outfits. We watch *The Mickey Mouse Club* at Kip's. Afterward, we always do the Mouseketeer roll call.

"Wallace, get out of bed! I think I see Kip coming up the driveway." Actually, that's not really true. He's not here yet, but it always works.

Wallace throws back the covers and stands up on her bed and says, "Brrrrr, did the stove go out?"

"Come on, Wallace," I say, "hurry and change your clothes."

(Wallace was too tired last night to put on her pajamas, so she slept in her dress.)

"No," says Wallace, "I'm way too cold. I'm going to put on another dress on top of this dress."

"You can't do that, Wallace."

"Yes, I can. Heidi did it," says Wallace, going to her closet area and pulling out a pink dress with gray poodles and Eiffel Towers all over the skirt. That dress used to be mine, and before that it was our cousin Candy Clark's, who lives in Milton, Massachusetts. She sent us a huge box of her summer dresses with crinoline slips and matching organdy jackets.

"Wallace, you can't wear two dresses. You'll look fat."

Our mother is out by the stove, trying to get the fire going. The room is full of smoke. She's waving a newspaper in the air. I look out the window, and now I really do see Kip sitting on a big tree stump out in front waiting for us. "Wallace, hurry!"

We're supposed to take turns fixing the lunch boxes, but Wallace hardly ever does her turn. Anyway, when she fixes the lunch boxes, I get all sorts of weird stuff like crackers with pickles on them or olives mixed with strawberry jam on bread. So naturally you can guess who usually fixes the lunch boxes — me, or as we say in French class, "C'est moi!" I usually make peanut butter–and–mayonnaise sandwiches. Then if Wallace and I happened to have made a cake from a cake mix the day before, I cut a slice for each of us and wrap it up, also.

Actually, a couple of days ago we did make a cake. The package called it a Deluxe White Wedding Cake, but we decided to make our cake look like a swimming pool. We dropped blue food coloring in the mix and baked the cake in one flat pan. Then we decorated it with blue frosting and white patches for wave caps. That was Kip's idea. He came over at the end and was licking all the spoons and offering suggestions.

Then Wallace wanted to put Huckleberry Hound on the cake. "Wallace," I said, "why would Huckleberry Hound be in a swimming pool? Think about it." Then Wallace got mad and quit, and Kip was circling the table like a shark, looking at the cake. Wallace packed up her suitcase, and I think she was heading out for Seattle when I said, "Oh, okay, you can put Huckleberry Hound on *this* end of the pool *only.*"

So she did. She used dark blue and red food coloring, and she painted a big, purple dog on one end of the cake. "That's your part of the cake, Wallace," I said. "I'm not going to eat that big, purple thing."

Kip said he'd be glad to eat the Huckleberry Hound part and right now, in fact. So we cut some pieces off and went over by the woodstove and sat on the floor and ate the cake. It was really good.

"Too squishy for me," said our mother, as she sipped her Earl Grey tea, "and way too blue."

"Come on, Wallace. We're late," I call again, snapping the

lunch boxes closed. The room is smoky, and the fire is going in the stove. I can hear it hissing and puffing and crackling as it heats up.

"It's smoky because of the wind," our mother says, "but look how pretty the snow looks blowing around outside."

Wallace comes out of her room wearing two dresses and a coat. The underneath dress is a little longer, and I can see its hemline hanging down. She's got some notebooks and a lot of loose papers in her arms.

"Wallace, go in the kitchen and drink some juice," our mother says, throwing a small log into the stove.

Wallace meanders around the living room and into the kitchen area, singing a few bars of "I Wish I Were an Oscar Mayer Wiener." She stands at the kitchen table, closes her eyes, and says, "Ick." Then she drinks a small glass of orange juice in one gulp.

Wallace and I have some things in common. We both hate eating or drinking anything before school. We also both wear our hair in long braids, and we both desperately want to cut it. But our mother won't let us. We're the only kids in school with braids.

Wallace puts down her glass of juice and walks into the living area. "Mom," she says, "can I get my hair cut after school?" Wallace makes her first two fingers into a pair of fake scissors and clips an invisible path through the air.

"If you cut your hair, girls," our mother says, looking sadly at us this morning as she sits there in front of the woodstove, "then you'll just look like everybody else. Is that what you want?"

And Wallace says, "Yes, isn't that right, Fiona? We want to look like everybody else."

Our mother shakes her head as if she can't believe that, and then she dips back behind her book, *The Magical World of Roses*.

The door of the woodstove is open and I can see the orange fire leaping around in there like a caged tiger. Our mother shuts the stove door with her foot. She has on her fuzzy, brown slippers that look like bear paws.

We all got a pair of those slippers last Christmas, but Wallace ruined hers when she wore them outside in the rain. She stood in the orchard in the muddy wet grass when we were picking some apples to make applesauce one Sunday.

"Wallace," I said, "you're not supposed to wear your bear-paw slippers outdoors."

"Fiona, bears don't look out of their caves in the morning and go, 'Oh, I guess I won't go outside today, because it's raining and I don't want to get my feet muddy.' *That's* not what bears do, Fiona. *That* isn't the way bears are."

"Okay, Wallace, but you're wrecking your slippers," I said. She still wears them all the time anyway, even though they are weird and stiff-looking now and make a strange scratching sound when she walks around in them.

"Bye, Mom," Wallace says, looking back through the double doors. She stands there a moment as if she's waiting for something, and then she hurries off.

Sometimes it's hard to believe that our mother used to be constantly doing things. She used to work so hard on her sculpture that she usually had blisters and calluses on her hands. She would spend all day long pounding and carving in her studio. She usually wore a mask when she was polishing marble because of the fine dust it produced . . . dust like snow that sifted all over everything. If you went to her studio, you could tell where she had walked all day because of her footprints in the white marble dust.

When she finished a piece, she would say to my father, "William, I'm done, finally. Though I hate to be done. I always think I might make it even better if I keep going."

My father was very proud of my mother. He sold her sculptures in his galleries, not just in New York, but in London and Paris, too.

"Yes, I'm finally done with this one," she'd say. And then my father would put on Dinah Shore singing "I'll Be Seeing You." That was the song they listened to when they first met. One time my father asked my mother to dance even though her smock was covered in white marble dust. When they stopped dancing, my father looked down and started laughing because he had a white dust impression of my mother against his body.

"Bye, Mom," I say now, picking up my lunch box and closing the double doors behind me.

Our mother murmurs from behind her book, "Bye, girls," as if she barely hears me and is almost lost now in *The Magical World of Roses*.

Wallace hurries ahead of me, and by the time I get to the front door she's already in the big, empty room opposite the hallway. She's sitting on the edge of a pedestal underneath one of my mother's statues. The room is large around her, and standing above her is a pale-green statue of a woman holding a bouquet of carved-marble flowers. Wallace is leaning against the statue pretending to be asleep, snoring and then whistling, like they do in cartoons.

"Wake me up when we get there," she says with a groggy voice. I can see she has one eye partly open to watch my reaction. "And by the way, I beat you."

"Did I miss something? Was there a race?" I say.

"I'm *definitely* the winner this time," says Wallace, getting up. "I beat you to the door. I was *so* far ahead of you, I even had time to take a nap." Wallace yawns and stretches.

"I didn't hear any countdown. I didn't even know we were racing, Wallace," I say.

"Well, we were," says Wallace, "and I had a great nap. *That's* how far ahead I was."

Her voice echoes in the large, empty sitting room, a sitting room without chairs, a sitting room with a great, bowed window, where just outside dinner-plate dahlias used to bloom, a sitting room with a pink fireplace with broken lions holding up the mantel, a sitting room where my father used to visit with his friends. I can remember their names now: Bob Gifford, Ben Bowsma, Lon Bartlet, Don Mace, Bill Middleton. They were writers and artists and musicians and teachers. My father filled the house with paintings and music and books and antiques and friends.

"Oops, I forgot my book bag, but who cares?" says Wallace, crooking her neck, trying to watch Kip out there in the yard. He's whizzing back and forth, catching snowflakes with his tongue.

I go over to the front door and open it. A stream of snow rushes in. Some of the snowflakes catch a draft and float up, up the stairwell.

"Oh," says Wallace, spinning around, "the snow is falling up instead of down."

"Come on," Kip calls out, "I've caught two hundred and five snowflakes waiting for you two." They look pretty easy to catch. They are great, big flakes, and when they land on the orange leaves they remind me of the way sugar looks on Wheaties before you add the milk.

Wallace and I step out into the swirling, dizzying snow.

"If you stare straight up at the sky with the snow falling, you almost feel like you're going to faint," I say.

Wallace tilts her head back and starts staring at the sky, and then she says, "I did it and I didn't faint, Fiona. I didn't faint!" Wallace looks around and smiles.

Kip has left his big "dinner pail" on the tree stump. Kip calls his lunch box, which is black and curved on top, a dinner pail. Wallace and I think that's kind of funny.

"Don't forget your dinner pail," calls Wallace, running down the road, "and I'll be the first one to the bus stop!" Then the wind sweeps across the orchard and blows her armful of papers up and away, up and away into a lower field of tall, dry grass. We look up and see Wallace's papers sailing and twirling down with the snow, like white leaves falling from an enormous tree up in the sky. "My school project!" shouts Wallace.

As the papers fly above us, I can see some of them are drawings of dogs with big, floppy ears and others are charts with numbers on them. "Hurry," shouts Wallace. "Try to catch them!"

We run down into the field of tall, dry grass, but the wind is strong. Kip catches one page, a picture of a dog wearing a hat. "No, that's not my project. That's just a picture. Quick, catch my project." We run and we run, but the wind is ahead of us and blows Wallace's papers way to the edge of the field, over the drop-off, and down into the muddy, quick river that rushes way below. Kip catches another piece, a graph with a red line climbing up the page, but it's torn and wet, and the rest of the project is floating down the river into town.

Wallace sits down in the middle of the field full of tall, dry grass and she won't get up. She has some mud on her cheeks and there's snow all over her coat.

"Wallace!" we call out. "Come on. We'll miss the bus!" It's snowing these big flakes all around Wallace and you can barely see her sitting there lost in a sea of yellow grass. I forgot to brush her hair this morning because we were late, and right now she reminds me of one of those ponies we see not far from here that stay out in the field most of the year and have leaves and twigs tangled in their manes and tails.

"Wallace, come on!" we call. Kip and I run across the field to her. When we get there she's curled up in a ball down in the long grass, and when she sits up we see she's been crying.

"Come on, Wallace, it's only homework. It doesn't matter *that* much," I say.

Kip tugs on Wallace's braid and says, "Come on, Little Soldier. It doesn't matter." Kip's father calls Wallace "Little Soldier." She *loves* it, and whenever he comes over she always starts marching around calling out, "Hup, two, three, four. About face!"

That gets Wallace up, though she drags her feet and frowns at the sky. All three of us trudge quietly back across the field. It's hard to walk in really tall grass. It sweeps and moves all around you almost like water.

Finally we get back to the road. As we walk along, Wallace has her face down and is looking at her feet. "Now my teacher will say to me, 'Where's our class project?' And I'll have to say, 'It blew into the river and floated away.' "

"And I don't think she's going to believe you, Wallace," says Kip, picking up a stone and tossing it way back over the field toward the river.

CHAPTER VI

At Last, We get to the look-off point with the whole valley spread out below us. From the high ridge we can see the small group of children waiting in the cold for the bus at the bottom of the hill. They stand huddled in a circle, almost motionless. As we get closer, I recognize Wallace's friend Shorkey, all bundled up in a blue snowsuit, hat, and mittens. He's dressed for a blizzard. He has a scarf wrapped around his face, so I'm not even sure if Shorkey is in there at all.

"Hey, Wallace," I say as we pass the yellow willow tree that hangs over the road just before we get to the bus stop, "did you ever notice that you aren't the only one with the weird name? What about your friend Shorkey?"

"Oh, his real name is Christopher Shorkey," says Wallace. "Kids just call him Shorkey at school. And at home his Mom calls him 'Jelly Beans.' "

"I've got a cousin out in Deerlodge, Montana, who's a baby," says Kip. "And her mom works at the A&P, and she calls my cousin 'Little Rump Roast.' So you see, Wallace, what did I tell you?" says Kip, hurrying ahead of us. "Things could be worse."

Kip always hurries away when we get close to the bus stop. And at school I usually just say hi to Kip and that's it. He eats lunch with the other sixth-grade boys, and they end up throwing food. Kip gets a lot of attention for a routine he calls his "french-fry toss." He throws a french fry way high up to the ceiling and then he catches it in his mouth. He never misses. Wallace is always trying that trick, but she's never gotten it once. Kip can do peas, too. Thank goodness Wallace doesn't try peas.

When we get to the circle of kids at the bus stop, we sort of ease in next to Shorkey and an older boy, whose name we don't know. The older boy has a long neck with an Adam's apple on it that moves around whenever he says anything.

We turn toward Shorkey, who opens his lunch box and gets out a Pez dispenser, cranks Bugs Bunny's head back, and pops out a lemon Pez. He offers it to Wallace, saying, "You can have the whole thing. I've got two more dispensers at home. She brought me three after work last night. She's on the night shift at Buddy's Brushes, and they gave her three Pez dispensers because they thought she had three kids." He doesn't say who "she" is.

We look up and the bus is barreling around the corner through veils of whirling snow. When it comes to a stop, the folded bus door pulls open and Shorkey hops on, followed by

Wallace, who says to the driver, "In October I've never seen snow like this! It's not even Halloween, and it's snowing!"

Wallace sits with Shorkey, and I get in behind them next to my friend Nell, who has been on the bus for a while and looks warm and tired. Nell is wearing a clean, blue jacket and she has shiny, short hair that swings out from her head in a happy way whenever she moves. She has a small nose with eight freckles scattered over the top of it. Nell hates her freckles. We're always counting them to see if any have disappeared. Once I only counted six freckles and Nell started hopping around, saying, "They're fading. They're fading. Thank you! Thank you!" But it turned out I had forgotten the two on the tip of her nose.

Nell is the girl who gave me my pink leotard and a real pair of toe shoes for ballet that used to be hers. They are made of pink silk and they're hard around the toe area. You stuff them with lamb's wool, and then, once you find your balance, you are able to dance way up on the tips of your toes. It hurts, though. It looks very beautiful from the outside, but on the inside it hurts. I love my toe shoes. I have learned to use them and dance in our big ballroom early in the morning before anyone is awake at my house.

I once went with Nell to her ballet class downtown in a studio above the bakery. All the walls are mirrors, and all the dancers were working to be able to do splits, flat up against the wall with both legs. I can pretty much do that. I practice it all the time. Next, the dancers did certain steps down the length of the studio and back again. Then they did their positions at the barre, and the teacher played the piano. I longed to join in, but was only a visitor, not part of the class. I was watching from the seats at the back with someone's mother and little brother. I was really roasting in my coat, but I was too embarrassed to take it off. I didn't really want anyone to notice me sitting there. After class, Nell came over to me and said, "Your house or mine?"

I have been to Nell's house about a million times, but she has never been to my house. When she asks about coming over, I always tell her some story like "You can't come today because my grandmother is sick," even though my gram doesn't even live with us. I never want Nell to see my house or to know where I live. I'm sure if she did, she would never like me again.

Now the bus driver snaps the door shut, and Kip and the tall boy with the Adam's apple go way to the back. It's noisy back there, and a lot of the boys open the windows and throw things out or shout at cars going by. Some of the little kids are afraid to go to the back at all. You could get knocked down, or someone could steal your books.

Out the window now the bus is passing an Algonquin Indian burial ground, or a least it looks like one. Wallace found a bone there once, and we thought it was prehistoric or a dinosaur bone or an Indian bone, so we took it to school. Wallace thought she was going to sell the bone to a big museum and make tons of money. But things never work out that way. It turned out to be a recent cow bone, a front leg, with a fancy name like femuritis or something like that.

I open my book bag to make sure I have my homework, my report on Franklin Roosevelt. I think he was a great president, helping the poor, making things better for people. Next to me, Nell is writing a list of things for school on the palm of her hand. Nell writes on her palm a lot.

We're almost to school now. I can tell as we round the bend past a building with the words *Knights of Columbus* written above the door. After that is Buddy's Brush Factory, *Quality Paintbrushes for Quality Lives*. Wallace and Shorkey are turned around, sitting up on their knees, staring at me and Nell. They both have yellow Pez candy all over their mouths. "Yuck," says Nell. "How can you eat that stuff?"

Nell stands at the edge of the wooden gymnasium with her feet in first position on the painted white line that goes around the gym. We have about ten minutes to practice ballet before school starts. She puts her hands on her hips and leans her head down, breathing heavily. She just did a whole string of graceful dance steps, and now she's resting. I think Nell enjoys playing the teacher.

She puts her stocking feet in third position and does a port de bras and then adds on a pirouette. "Then it's fifth position with a turn like this," she says, sweeping into a delicate spin.

"Oh, like this," I say, and I get into fifth position and then I do the pirouette and then another and another.

"Fiona," says Nell, pushing her hair off her face and looking at me with very clear eyes, "you looked like a little bird. That was beautiful!"

Then we start laughing because Peter Collins walks into the gym and opens the door of the closet where the P. E. equipment is kept. He has a key on an official chain, and when he opens the door, a whole bunch of rubber dodgeballs and leather soccer balls come flying out, scattering all over the gym. Peter Collins doesn't get flustered. He swings around, scooping them up and tossing them back in the closet. Then he dribbles one ball out into the corridor and disappears.

"I can't believe that happened," says Nell as we put on our shoes and head across the gym, trying to walk lightly on the white line so we don't scratch the floor with our street shoes.

Out in the hall we see Wallace and her class filing to the library. (Wallace has Library Skills first period.) She's hanging at the back of the line, with Shorkey just ahead of her. Wallace still has a worried look on her face. Shorkey looks eager and friendly, hurrying along ahead of Wallace.

"Come on, Wallace," says Shorkey, "if you hurry we can sit near the rabbit cage."

"I'm thinking, so I can't hurry," says Wallace, looking down.

Nell and I wait while Wallace's class files by. Then Wallace looks up and sees me and starts waving wildly, as if she didn't just see me ten minutes ago.

During History, our teacher, Miss Johnson, says, "Okay, class, I want you to pick a historical building in town and do a report. Any building will do. For instance, the Nokawa Community Library, which was built in 1840."

Billy Framboise raises his hand. "I'll do that one," he says. Miss Johnson writes his name on the blackboard.

Then Chester Bruce stands up and says, "How about that big, old mansion up on the hill overlooking the river? It's full of all these dark shadows and my mom says it used to be real nice. One time my mom went up there with a chocolate cake, because she felt sorry for them after what happened, and the woman wouldn't invite her in, and she wasn't friendly." Chester Bruce always stands up when he talks, and then he sits down abruptly and scoots his chair in tightly under his desk.

Miss Johnson looks over at me and then she looks down. I open the top of my desk and start rummaging around for papers. I don't want anyone to see me blush or cry.

But thank goodness Miss Johnson says, "No, Chet. We're only doing buildings in town for our City Planning section. The

Bryer Mansion that you are referring to is out in the country, so it's off-limits."

After Cathy Newton, it's my turn. Miss Johnson looks over at me and softly says, "Fiona Hopper, which building did you choose to do?"

"I guess I'll do mine on the building on Route 23 across from Buddy's Brush Factory, the Ho-hum Motel and Summer Cabins," I say, and then I look around the room at all the smiling, happy faces. I wonder if they would still be smiling at me if they knew that I was part of the family that lives up on the hill with all those shadows.

CHAPTER VII

After school Nell and I walk downtown to the dance studio. As we are walking we are kicking a stone along the sidewalk. It's new cement and impressions from leaves float on the surface in a few squares. One square has squirrel tracks running across it. A flock of geese in a great **V** fly overhead. I can hear them squawking and calling as they fly. It seems to me they must be crying out to each other, "Wait for me! Wait for me! Hey, wait for me!" It stopped snowing earlier today, but I wonder how geese would fly through that. How could they navigate in all that whiteness?

Nell is just saying, "As a matter of fact, I suppose you could have those, too."

"Those what?" I ask.

"Those extra tights of mine. I just got a new pink pair."

"Sure," I say, trying to sound casual. Actually, I'd love to have a pair of tights to go with the leotards, and I love the chance to visit Nell's dance studio. We pass the bakery now, and the window is full of the most beautiful cookies and pies and cakes.

There are rows of cherry tarts and plates of yellow bonbons. Just beyond the bakery is the door to the dance studio, and we push it open and start to climb the stairs.

Right away I hear the piano playing. It's a tinkling, trailing sound, and I hear the floor thumping with dancers' leaps. It's hard to explain, and I know it seems odd, but I love this sound. It's a sound that gives me a happy, Christmas kind of feeling.

Once we get upstairs, I follow Nell across the polished wood floor. We seem to be barging in on a class, but Nell is not concerned, and so I follow her. The teacher stops playing the piano for a moment, saying, "People, people, people, not so quickly. You rushed through the part. Slow it down, even more, much slower."

The teacher has an accent. She is from Cuba. "A dancer who also plays the piano," said Nell on the way over, in the hushed voice she always uses when she talks about her teacher. "Isn't that neat?"

"Look," says the teacher now, "Geniveve, did you practice yesterday?"

"Not really," says Geniveve, "I was sick."

"Look," says the teacher, still sitting at the piano. "Did you know that I left my country, Cuba, a year ago because Castro took my house and my family's land? So I moved to a small apartment and my piano was the only thing I really owned other than my clothes. Did you know it took up the whole one-roomed apartment? Finally, I told the government that I wanted to leave and live in America. That very day the soldiers came to take my piano away from me. They came with an army truck and an enormous crane, and they arrested my piano and lifted it out over the yard and through the air. The children in the neighborhood watched in a row, as if they were at a puppet show. I stood by a yucca tree. I remember the shadows on the ground, Geniveve. They reminded me of spears stabbing, as I watched my piano leaving, flying away from me, being taken from me by soldiers like a prisoner.

"Do you know how hard it has been to leave my country and come to America, to this little town, to this little dance studio? Hard work, Geniveve. It has been hard work. When I ask you to practice, Geniveve, please practice. I'll do my part, and you do yours." She starts playing the piano again after that speech, saying, "From the beginning, and slowly."

I follow Nell across a wall of mirrors at the other end of the studio. Then we pass in front of a separate oval mirror in a gold frame on a stand. Nell whispers to me, "She was a principal dancer in Cuba. She danced Giselle in a performance attended by General Batista before he was overthrown."

As we pass the oval mirror that faces the wall of mirrors, I see myself and Nell, repeated and repeated and repeated into infinity. A million mes and a million Nells that go on into forever.

Nell opens her locker now and drags out a dangling pair of black tights. She tosses them and they come flying at me like a dark bird.

"I would give anything to be in that class," I tell Nell as we open the door at the bottom of the stairs and step out into the street. We round the corner and the wind hits our faces, blows our coats and scarves up and back. I shout against the wind, "And I'd give anything to be in the Christmas recital. Anything!"

Nell lives a few blocks from downtown on a little street off Main. All the lawns here look like green rugs. They probably don't ever need mowing. The bushes are so pretty, all clipped and shaped, so they don't even look real to me. They remind me of the little, green bushes on Kip's Lionel train set-up. To make those bushes, Kip uses baby-bottle brushes and cuts them down, paints them green, and makes little stands for them. He uses dried peas to make the stonework on the outside of the little buildings. Where the train stops, he made a hotel called Kip's Plaza out of dried green peas set into plaster of paris. Then he painted the whole thing, and it looks just like a stone building.

Nell's street is called Jane Street. I really like that name. It's so easy to remember and has an average sound to it. As if nothing out of the ordinary ever happens here. If you live on Jane Street, you're bound to have tons of friends, a bunch of golf clubs in your garage, and a happy, safe life where no one ever dies. I wish we lived on Jane Street.

Wallace knows a little girl who lives two doors down in a house that looks a lot like Nell's house. Wallace doesn't go over there very often because the little girl calls her "Walrus." As we walk past her house now, the little girl is in her yard trying to hula hoop with her coat on, which you can't do. She calls out, "Where's Walrus?"

And I just say, "Who's that?" and we keep on walking.

At Nell's house, Nell pushes open the front door, and we walk in on her fluffy wall-to-wall carpeting. It's so soft you can't hear the sound of our feet. Everything is muffled. Even the door as it shuts is muffled, almost mute. A clean, fluffy cat, white as the white carpeting, waits at the bottom of the stairs. Nell picks him up and says, "Mooshy, oh, look at you. Look at him, isn't he sweet? He's been declawed because he scratched the davenport in my dad's den."

At our house we say couch instead of davenport. Nell's mother is always saying, "Nell, take your feet off the davenport." At our house no one says anything about not putting our feet up on the couch. And we don't use the word *den*. We don't even know what it is. We kind of like the idea though, and once

Wallace wanted everyone to call her bedroom the den. She put up signs that said *Welcome to the den* and *This den belongs to Wallace Hopper.* I wouldn't do it, but Kip was willing, and when he'd come over, he'd say, "Is Wallace in her den?"

"Not *her* den . . . *the* den," Wallace would call from her room.

And then Kip would say, "Touchy, touchy, touchy."

Now Nell and I stand in the hallway patting Mooshy and looking at the little, pink pads on the bottom of his feet and feeling where he used to have claws. Nell puts him down, and he makes no sound at all as he walks across the carpet. Everything here seems to float as if two inches off the ground, all puffy and hushed and comfortable, and I feel I should be whispering. We go into her living room and sit down on a couch (davenport) that is soft and deep and silent, also. There are TV trays stacked there and a magazine stand with a *Life* magazine on it with President Kennedy on the cover. He's on his sailboat, and the wind is rippling through his hair.

Kenny, Nell's little brother, comes running into the living room and snaps on the small TV and shouts, "I'M watching *Spin and Marty.* So there!"

"Fine," says Nell, "no one's stopping you. Come on, Fiona. Let's get out of here."

I follow Nell into her bedroom. On all her walls are pictures of ballet dancers. There is a poster of Margot Fonteyn and Rudolf Nureyev in "Romeo and Juliet." He's holding her as she does an arabesque. There are some photographs of Nell in her first recital. She looks about five or six. I hardly recognize her because she still had her baby teeth then, and her smile looked different.

"My grandmother was a ballerina," I tell Nell, "and she gave me a music box with a dancer on the top."

Nell tilts her head and smiles. She runs her hand over the white, crocheted bumps on a new bedspread on her bed. "My mom just finished this. It's the popcorn stitch," she says.

Leaning against the fluffy pillows on the bed is an autograph dog — a long, blue dachshund with autographs written all over his body. I pick it up to read them and find the autograph I put on there last spring written on the long flap of his ear. It says *To Nell, a great kid. Keep up the dancing. Fiona.*

Everyone in our school has signed the dog. An autograph from Peter Collins says *The oak tree is strong, its branches straight and true. Remember the mighty oak tree was once a nut like you. Signed, the great me, Peter C.*

"Is that when you used to like him?" I ask.

"Shut up," says Nell.

I find Wallace's signature across the back of the dog. It takes up a huge amount of space and just says *W A L L A C E* in funny-looking, big letters.

And then Kip wrote, on the leg of the dog, *When you dance in New York, Nell, I hope you'll stay at my five-star hotel on Park Ave. Sincerely yours, Kipton Jones.*

On the dog's head, the ballet teacher, Miss Carmen Estrellada, wrote in sweeping, curling letters *For little Nell, who dances like a butterfly.*

"Do you know what I heard her name means in Spanish?" says Nell, looking at me with her serious, green eyes. "I heard it means 'sky full of stars.' Isn't that amazing? Miss Carmen Estrellada is the most beautiful dancer. She did a small part in our recital last year. She hasn't gotten married yet because her fiancé was killed in Cuba. He was hit by a car. On that day, September third, Miss Estrellada always wears the same dress she wore that day she ran to find him. It's torn and even has her fiancé's bloodstains on the hem. She wears it every year on September third. She wears it to class and then all day and into the evening," says Nell, putting the autograph dog back against the pillow.

"Gee whiz," I say, and then Nell and I go on to talk about other things like the Algonquin Indian basket we're making in school and the spelling test we had before lunch, where we had to write out the pledge of allegiance to the flag and spell words like *indivisible*, which no one got right, not even Ed Brown, who always gets everything right.

While we are talking, Nell's little brother, Kenny, keeps running by the room and shooting at us with his cap gun (no caps in it). Nell calls out, "Quit it, Kenny. Go outside." But he doesn't pay any attention and keeps darting back and forth across the door. "Can you believe," says Nell, "he's named Ken and he's nothing like Ken from Barbie and Ken? He's like the complete opposite. Cut it out, Kenny," she says again, and then she rushes up to the door and smooshes it shut, because nothing in this house slams.

After a while, the door opens just a crack and poking through is the long, shiny barrel of a .45 caliber. "MOM," shouts Nell, "Kenny is bugging us." I know her mother can't hear her, because I can see her mother outside through the window. She's at the clothesline, with a great, white sheet billowing in her arms.

At five o'clock we get to have dinner. I never heard of eating so early. We get to have chicken pot pies, and we get to use the TV trays. On each tray there's a picture of a deer standing in a marshy field. We set up the trays on their little legs in front of the couch and place our dinners on the trays. Kenny is in the kitchen eating with his parents. From here, I can see they have a baby gate across the door to keep the cat in the kitchen.

Nell and I are watching a great show on TV. It's called *The Millionaire,* and it starts off with the millionaire seen from the back, writing a check for a million dollars. You never see his face. Then the story goes on to show who got the million dollars — usually a very poor but nice person, and they never knew who gave them the money, or why. It's a great show, even though you never get to see the millionaire's face.

During a commercial break, watching an ad for White Rain shampoo, Nell says, "On Halloween we're having a party at the ballet studio and Miss Carmen Estrellada is going to announce the theme and story of our Christmas recital. I'm going to ask her, when I get up the nerve, if you can try out for it. I'm going to tell her that I taught you all the steps, and that you practice all the time."

I take a bite of the chicken pot pie. It tastes so warm and delicious, and it's so much fun sitting at the TV tray tables, trying to guess what the millionaire will do next, after the commercial.

After dinner Nell's father, Mr. Stamford, drives me home. Nell's mother says Nell has to have a bath and do her homework, so she can't go along. Nell folds her arms and looks away, and then she stomps into the house and shuts the door without even saying goodbye. Mr. Stamford and I go into the garage, which is full of bicycles, basketballs, hockey skates, golf clubs, picnic coolers, and an old Brownie uniform that Nell wore before she flew up to Girl Scouts.

We get in the big car with the scratchy seats, and Mr. Stamford starts the motor. He turns on the windshield wipers, as a slight, misty rain is starting to fall. He backs the car out and drives slowly down the street, the windshield wipers sloshing across the window. The downtown area is pretty much dark and closed up, except for the newspaper-and-candy store. I can see

Marty Pippin in there closing out the cash register. Marty Pippin's wife is Mrs. Pippin, the fifth-grade teacher at our school, and whenever the kids in that class get 100 on a spelling test, they get a package of Necco Wafers. Lucky ducks.

Because of the cold and the rain, it seems like everyone else has gone home. Mr. Stamford snaps the radio on and then off and heads up the hill outside of town now. It's very quiet inside the car, and I can even hear the motor working to pull us up the hill.

"What grade are you in?" asks Mr. Stamford.

"Ah, sixth grade, the same as Nell," I say. I add an *ah*, because the answer doesn't seem long enough without it.

"Oh, okay," says Mr. Stamford.

We curve around through the fields of corn stubble and then past a stand of trees and a picnic table. Once Kip and I and Wallace walked to that spot and had a picnic lunch. Actually, Wallace didn't walk. We pulled her the whole way there in a red wagon.

Mr. Stamford gets to the bottom of my road, where our mailbox is. "You can stop here," I tell Mr. Stamford. "I can walk up the rest of the way. It's way too slippery, you'd never make it up the hill."

Mr. Stamford stops the car. "This isn't the road that goes by that big, old place, is it? You know the one I mean, the one that used to be real nice, where that incident occurred, oh, four, five years ago?"

"Oh, no, no," I answer quickly, "that must be the next road up."

I get out of the car and lean through the window. "Thank you, Mr. Stamford. Tell Nell I'll see her tomorrow, and thank you." I always say thank you at least twice. It's just a habit of mine. My mother says I should only say thank you once. "Quit saying thank you all the time," she says. But it's better than Wallace, who never says thank you at all.

Mr. Stamford's car pulls away, and I'm left in the rainy darkness. I knew the snow we had this morning would be mostly gone. It was what you call a freak snowstorm.

I like walking in the rain in the dark. I can think about things, about Miss Carmen Estrellada running toward her fiancé in Cuba and about Franklin and Eleanor Roosevelt and the ocean surf pounding near their house on Campobello Island.

I pass the road to Kip's trailer. In the dark in the woods, I can see the light from the windows and Kip's TV flickering. He and his father are probably watching *Perry Mason*. Kip's father can always figure out that show before it's half over.

I pass a stand of pine trees that represents the beginning of our property. They are so dark and tall and blow together in the wind, making a rushing sound. As I get into our yard, I can see that the huge house is all dark, except for the wing to the left, where we live. The windows in that huge room are lit up like a candle in the night. One window is tall and wide and has many panes. I can see Wallace sitting there, with her face pushed against the glass, watching for me. I can tell by the way she's sitting there that she has been waiting a long time.

Chapter VIII

"Good thing we're working on our Halloween outfits *now*," I said to Wallace, who was running a little to keep up with me as we headed toward the downtown. "Some kids wait till the last minute and then they just throw on any old thing. That's why there are so many ghosts out there on Halloween night."

"Yeah, remember last year?" said Wallace, leaping over a crack in the sidewalk. "Kip couldn't think of a costume and then at the last minute he ended up going as a baked potato, with tinfoil wrapped all over his body. He even got second prize at the Knights of Columbus Halloween party!"

"That was because of his acting skills, Wallace. He didn't just *look* like a baked potato, he *acted* like one."

"Yeah," said Wallace, taking a deep breath and looking around at everything.

We passed Marty Pippin's newspaper-and-candy store and then a little restaurant, called The Nokawa Nugget, with a big coffee cup painted on the window, a painted swirl of white steam curling above the cup. Just across the street was the bakery and, on the second floor, Miss Carmen Estrellada's dance studio. I looked up for a moment and then looked away.

Wallace took the opportunity to jump ahead of me. She pushed open the swinging doors of the dime store and just about knocked over a little kid in a pumpkin mask. Then she zipped past the 45 records, past the coloring books and paper dolls, and she stopped in front of the shelf full of Halloween costumes. All week Wallace had had her eye on a store-bought skeleton outfit where the skeleton glows in the dark.

"It's really scary," Wallace said. "That's the one I want." It was in a box next to a Glinda of Oz outfit with glitter stars all over the skirt and a cape with Munchkins all over it and a magic wand, but Wallace said, "I'll take the skeleton," and she sat down on the wooden floor of the dime store.

"Wallace, get off the floor," I said. "Here comes Peter Collins from school."

Wallace wouldn't get up. "I'm too tired," she said.

Peter Collins hurried through, looked at the costumes, picked up a Mars bar, dropped a nickel on the counter, and left. He has such a casual, sure way about him. Of course, he didn't say hello to us; besides, we were pretending to look at the ceiling at the time.

Wallace was now lying on the floor on her stomach, twirling a little metal top she pulled out of a five-cent bin. "Five ninety-nine . . . Why five ninety-nine? . . . Why not six dollars or five dollars? . . . Why five ninety-nine?" she said, spinning the little top.

"It doesn't matter," I said. "You don't have the money anyway, Wallace. Look at this yo-yo. It's a ghoulish Halloween yo-yo with a jack-o-lantern on it, and it's only twenty-nine cents. We can buy this." I'm pretty good at yo-yoing. I can do "walking the dog" and "around the world," and I can sleep a yo-yo for hours.

I was spinning it to get it started when Wallace sat up, pulled off one of her shoes, took off a long, blue sock, and dumped four quarters and a crumpled five-dollar bill out of it.

"Where did you get that, Wallace?" I asked her.

"My friend gave it to me," said Wallace. "My friend Mrs. Braverman gave me the money so I could be a store-bought skeleton."

At the counter, the dime-store owner took Wallace's crumpled money and put her skeleton outfit in a bag. I bought some red wax lips with sweet syrup inside them and a box of Milk Duds. I was going to save the Milk Duds for lunch the next day, but Wallace pestered me on the way home until I got them out.

Halfway up Main Street we always like to stop in the little park where there's a real cannon. Underneath it there's a plaque that says *In Honor of the Bravery of the Men in World War II.* We sat down on a cement ledge, and Wallace ran her fingers over the list of men who died in battle. We sat there eating Milk

Duds, watching the squirrels running around in the park and the leaves gathering in the wind under the trees.

A policeman walked by. It was Officer Wolf McKane. He said, "Wallace and Fiona, how are you doing? I haven't see you two in a while."

When I saw his face I got kind of dizzy and I felt like I wanted to go home.

"We're fine. Aren't we, Wallace?" I said, pulling on her arm. "It's time to go home. Come on."

Wallace dropped a few Milk Duds and then she frowned at me, her eyes matching the rainy-looking sky behind her.

We're up in the ballroom now with Kip, working on our Halloween costumes. It's late afternoon and a soft, blurry rain washes over the French doors at the back of the ballroom.

Wallace keeps standing up and shaking her fist at the window and saying, "Stop raining. Right now. Stop." She wants it to stop because in a few hours we'll be out trick-or-treating.

I'm sewing a button on part of my costume, but I stop for a minute and look out through the windows and wonder how Miss Carmen Estrellada's ballet party will go tonight. Will it be at her dance studio or at her house? Will everyone be in costume, including Miss Carmen Estrellada? I wish I could go. I know tonight Miss Estrellada will announce the theme and story for the Christmas recital. Nell was so excited. She couldn't wait to find out what it was going to be.

I try to imagine what the recital will be like. I lie back on the ballroom floor and look at the walls all around this room. There are clusters of plaster cherubs in each corner, among swirls of flowing ribbons. The cherubs are reaching for little plaster birds that flutter above them. Some of the plaster is broken in places, so one cherub is reaching for nothing at all.

It turns out that Kip and I have decided on a combination costume. We are going as Franklin and Eleanor Roosevelt. Kip brought up a wheelchair that had been his grandmother's, and he has these wire-framed glasses and his father's big, gray overcoat and a necktie with records all over it.

I'm wearing a hat my mother wore when she got engaged about a billion years ago. It's a pretty red color with pink flowers on the side, and it looks like the big hats Eleanor Roosevelt used to wear. Then I have clunky high heels that look like Minnie Mouse shoes and a big, old-fashioned coat. The coat is great, because it's cold out and it's so dumb to be dressed up in a real neat outfit and then put your regular coat over it so no one knows you're a gypsy or a nurse, because your coat covers up your costume.

Kip sits in the wheelchair, and I push him around the ballroom. I push real hard and fast, and he goes flying across the room, bumps against the little stage, and flops out on the floor and pretends to be dead. Like I said, Kip's *always* pretending to be dead.

"You're crying wolf, Kip," says Wallace. "Someday when you really *are* dead, we won't believe you. We'll be making wisecracks and jokes and stuff and you'll really be dead."

Kip lies there looking white as a ghost.

"Come on, Kip," says Wallace, "get up."

"Water," whispers Kip, "water, I need water." His voice sounds shaky and far away. "Waaater, quick. I'm dying. This is my last request. Please bring me waaa . . ."

Wallace hurries into the bathroom at the top of the staircase and rushes back in with a green, plastic tumbler of water. She lifts Kip's head up and pours water into his mouth.

He takes a big gulp, sits up, smiles, and says, "Thanks, Wallace. I was thirsty!"

Kip is really looking forward to collecting a lot of "loot" tonight, as he calls it. He always gets the most candy, because he's so persistent. He doesn't give up. If someone doesn't answer the bell, he waits, and he tries again. A lot of little kids give up right away if no one answers the door. They figure, *Oh, there's a better place around the corner.* That's why they never have much candy at the end of the night. But not Kip. He goes back later if he doesn't get a reply. Last year he took a huge Robert Hall shopping bag, and he filled the whole thing with candy. In fact, he told me last year he was the only trick-or-treater on the streets at eleven o'clock at night. Kip got so much candy last year that he was eating Halloween candy through Christmas and even into spring. I know because I saw a couple of marshmallow witches in his dinner pail last April.

Now as we set out trick-or-treating tonight, we are officially Eleanor Roosevelt in high heels, Franklin Roosevelt in a wheelchair, and a store-bought glow-in-the-dark skeleton walking down the dark hill into town. I'm pushing Kip in the wheelchair. But it's impossible on the dirt road, so Kip gets out and pushes it himself, and then the skeleton gets in and then won't get out later.

At the bottom of the first hill, among the fields where the road flattens out for a while, we have to wait while the six o'clock train goes through. We love to count the cars. We had one go through here once with two hundred and ninety cars. That was the longest one we've had. Kip's favorite car is the *Mohawk Central,* because Kip likes anything Indian. He always waits to see those cars. I like to see cars that say *The Wabash* on them, because I like the song "The Wabash Cannonball." We wait to see whose favorite car comes first. It's kind of a contest. Wallace's favorite car is one she saw last year. It said *The Burlington Zephyr* on it. Zephyr the monkey is her favorite animal in the Babar books, so that's her favorite train car. We only saw it that one time, but Wallace is still waiting.

"Maybe I'll see the *Burlington Zephyr* tonight," says Wallace.

"You're on a losing streak, Wallace. You need to pick a new horse," says Kip, patting Wallace on the back.

As the train approaches, the engineer sees us in our Halloween outfits, the Roosevelts and the skeleton, and he pulls his whistle, and we are swept away by the wind the train makes and the thunder of its wheels clacking along the tracks and the long, whining whistle. We stand there counting the cars and waiting to see the caboose. Most cabooses are red, but we've seen yellow ones and brown ones and green ones.

"That's the same engineer who waved to us last week," I shout as the train thunders by.

"No, it's not," says Wallace. "This engineer is much fatter and looks really cheerful. The other engineer didn't smile."

"Remember that time, Wallace, when we saw that engineer eating at the bakery?" I say.

"Yeah," says Wallace, "he was having a cheeseburger, and he was wearing an engineer's outfit and an engineer's hat and everything. I think he was Casey Jones."

"That wasn't Casey Jones, Wallace. Think about it. Why would Casey Jones come to this little town, even if he wasn't dead, which he is?"

"Well, he looked like Casey Jones," says Wallace.

"You should have gotten proof," says Kip. "You should have taken a photograph."

"I didn't have a camera," says Wallace, throwing her hands up into the night air.

After the train has passed, we are left standing in silence. With the excitement of the train gone, the night seems suddenly dark and lonely. We walk on through the corn stubble at the side of the road. We can hear the train whistle blowing in the distance as it passes the station in town across from the feed store and grain elevator. We head for a group of houses lit up farther down along the road. One has a jack-o-lantern burning on its porch.

"Every house is a little world," says Kip.

"Let's sneak up and look," says Wallace.

"That's illegal," I say.

"Kids don't get arrested," says Wallace. "Come on."

We follow Kip around to the side of one house and peer in through the white nylon curtains. A man is sitting in a chair with his feet on a footstool. The man is watching *It Could Be You* on television. The announcer is just calling out, "IT COULD BE YOU—MRS. JANE CARL!" The camera pans the audience and focuses on Mrs. Jane Carl, who is all excited and crying and laughing and everything.

"Come right up here, Mrs. Jane Carl," says the announcer. I

know this program. They will bring out all these people Mrs. Jane Carl knew when she was a kid.

The man watching TV gets up and goes to the kitchen and comes back with a bottle of Pal orange-ade and sits back down again. We creep around to the front of his house and ring the man's doorbell. He comes to the door with a plate of candied apples — apples on sticks standing in a pool of caramel.

"Trick or treat," we say, and he holds out the plate, and we each take a sticky apple. I'm the only one who says thank you. I try to give Kip a hint by nudging him in the rib cage, but he only says, "Cut it out, Fiona. You almost made me drop my candy."

As we walk away into the darkness, we can still hear the crowd clapping, and Mrs. Jane Carl sort of crying. Wallace can't get at her candied apple because she won't take off her mask. "No," says Wallace, "someone might see, and then they won't think I'm really a skeleton. You're supposed to keep your mask on. My teacher told me."

"The houses here are pretty small," says Kip, swinging his shopping bag of candy. We haven't gone far, so you can hear the Mars bar, two lollipops, and one Oh Henry! sliding around in there. "These houses are not big like the Wallace Hotel, but you can't tell by the size of the house how big the candy is going to be. I've had some very small houses give out great big PayDay bars."

"It's not a hotel," says Wallace.

"Someday it will be," says Kip, swinging his bag higher and higher. Wallace is pushing the empty wheelchair along through the rocks. "Someday," says Kip, "I'm going to fix up the whole house and put bell pulls on thick braided cords in every room, and then bellhops will be hopping all over the place with trays of cake and glasses of champagne. Everyone in the whole state will flock to the Wallace Hotel, and you can be one of the bellhops, Wallace."

"Yeah," says Wallace.

"And Fiona can be the ballerina in the lounge."

"*I* want to be the ballerina in the lounge," says Wallace. "Only not at our house. We hate our house. Don't we, Fiona?"

"Yup," I say, "we do."

"It's all broken and everything. Nobody would want to stay there, or if they did, they wouldn't pay any money," says Wallace, breathing loudly behind her mask.

We walk along in the dark, and finally Wallace throws her candied apple into the weeds at the side of the road. Soon we get to the edge of town, where there are sidewalks and street lamps and lots of houses to stop at. We begin to see other trick-or-treaters. Peter Collins, who isn't dressed up at all, is up on a porch with Alison Elkhart, who's about two feet taller than he is. Just as we're turning up that sidewalk, we run into Nell and her little brother, Kenny. Kenny is dressed in green army fatigues with a green army cap. He has paint on his cheeks, and he's carrying a great, big, plastic machine gun. He points the barrel at Wallace and says, "Hand over that candy or I'll shoot you."

"I'm not scared," says Wallace. "That gun is a fake."

Nell is dressed as a flamenco dancer. She has a big, red paper flower in her hair and bright-red lipstick on her lips and rouge on her cheeks. "Look, Fiona, at what Miss Carmen Estrellada gave me," she says, whispering to me. She shows me a chocolate ballerina covered with cellophane wrapping tied with a blue ribbon. "I'll keep it forever," she whispers. "I'll never even take a bite." The cellophane catches the light as she turns it around in her hand.

"I guess you had the party," I say. "Did Miss Carmen Estrellada tell you what the recital is going to be?"

Nell's eyes glisten under her powdery eye shadow. *"Yes,"* she says. "It's a secret. We're not supposed to tell anyone." She lowers her voice. "It's dedicated to Miss Carmen Estrellada's fiancé, the one who died. It's called 'The Dance of the Winter Moon.' Miss Carmen Estrellada says it's about flowers blooming in the winter and loving someone even when they're gone. The music is beautiful. She played it for us tonight."

Suddenly I turn around with my back to Nell and start quickly pawing through my bag of candy. I turn my head away and I don't want to look up.

"What are you doing, Fiona?" Nell asks.

"Umm, do you want a Snickers bar?" I say, tossing it up in the air.

"Yeah, I've only got about a billion in my bag," says Nell, laughing.

Then Nell's mother pulls up behind Nell and Kenny in their big, white station wagon. The headlights shine at the back of Nell's head almost like a halo. Nell puts the chocolate ballerina down into her shopping bag and says, "I have to go. See you in school on Monday." They drive off to another neighborhood, Nell waving from the back seat, like a flamenco dancer being taxied off to a performance.

Wallace and Kip and I head up the hill past a white church, all of us pushing the wheelchair together. We turn onto a street that runs along the top of the hill. Most of the houses are big up here and have longer yards that slope with the hill. At a big, white house with four jack-o-lanterns on the steps, Wallace says, "Let's go here, to Mrs. Braverman's. This is where she lives."

Wallace walks up the steps and rings the bell, as if she were at home here. "Hello, Mr. Braverman," she says to the man who answers the door. "I know you think there's a skeleton at your door, but really it's Wallace Hopper," she says. "And he isn't re-ally crippled at all. That's Kip."

"Wallace, come in," says Mr. Braverman, "and bring your friends with you."

"She's not my friend, she's my sister," says Wallace.

We drag the wheelchair up the steps and then once inside the warm, bright house, Kip leaps back into the chair and puts on his long, solemn, presidential face.

Mr. Braverman brings out several plates of treats — popcorn balls wrapped individually in waxed paper and a big bowl of candy corn and Double Bubble gum (our favorite). "Help yourself," says Mr. Braverman. "Mrs. Braverman is upstairs in the atrium with all the birds. She loves birds, doesn't she, Wallace? Mrs. Braverman has leukemia. She's rather frail, I'm sorry to say. But she's made all these lovely popcorn balls for you. Wallace will take you upstairs to visit Mrs. Braverman," says Mr. Braverman, putting a log on the glowing fire in the fireplace. The fireplace is pretty, covered in tiles, each tile a little picture — a windmill, a Dutch girl in wooden shoes, a cow standing in a field.

"Come on," says Wallace. "My friend Mrs. Braverman is upstairs."

Mr. Roosevelt leaves his wheelchair and pretends to lean on me for support. I lock my arm around his, and as we climb the stairs, a happy feeling comes over me.

Wallace knows the way. She's bouncing up the stairs, hopping twice on each step, taking forever. Finally, we get to the top, and down the hall, and then Wallace opens a large, oak double door. "Ssshh," she says. "This is the atrium. Hurry in and close the door behind you."

Inside the atrium, there is a huge, glass dome for a ceiling. There are all sorts of trees growing in big, clay pots, and there are baskets of ferns and palm trees and olive trees and azalea bushes, and all among the trees are birds. There are green and yellow parakeets that fly across the huge room. There is a white cockatoo that sits on a branch of an azalea bush. There is a whole tree of tiny, orange-and-black birds. The atrium is noisy with the sound of birds singing.

"Look who's here, Patsy," Mrs. Braverman says to a small, green parrot with a scissor tail and a big, orange beak. "Look who's here! It's Wallace Hopper. Patsy's not afraid of a glow-in-the-dark skeleton, are you, Patsy?"

Patsy says, "Pretty bird. Pretty bird."

Kip waves his arm in the air and a whole treeful of the tiny orange-and-black birds lift and flutter and scatter to bushes on the other side of the atrium. Patsy squawks, "Pretty bird. Pretty bird."

Mrs. Braverman hands Wallace the talking green parrot, saying, "There you go, go to Wallace. Tell Wallace all about it."

Wallace sits down, and the parrot nuzzles its head against her arm. Mrs. Braverman smiles at them with a sweet "good-bye" look, the kind of look people always seem to have at train stations when they're waving good-bye to someone as the train pulls away.

"Patsy, pretty bird," says Wallace.

Mrs. Braverman goes to the window. It's a big window, like at our house, with many small panes. She turns her back to us and looks up at the dark sky full of blinking stars. "They never could figure out the mystery of the universe, Wallace. They just never could figure it out, not all the king's horses or all the king's men," says Mrs. Braverman.

CHAPTER IX

I didn't ask Nell much about Miss Carmen Estrellada's party. She hurried away before I had a chance. Anyway, I pretty much figured no one would want a kid to be in a Christmas performance when the kid wasn't even in the class to begin with. I thought about it a little bit while we were out trick-or-treating, and when we got home late, I was surprised when I got a phone call.

Kip and Wallace and I were lying on the floor in our living area, separating out our candy into "most favorite" pile, "second most favorite" pile, and "least favorite" (possible candidates for trading) pile. Kip was just offering Wallace five root-beer barrels and four candy-corn pumpkins in return for her miniature Almond Joy bar, and Wallace was holding firm, when the telephone rang. I went over to the back wall next to the dark-green marble statue of a father with a smiling child riding on his shoulders. I reached across its polished surface to answer the phone.

It was Nell. Her voice sounded radiant, the way a shooting

star might sound if you could hear it whirling through the sky. "I got the part of the Camellia Princess," said Nell. "Miss Carmen Estrellada just called me."

"There were tryouts?" I said.

"Not really. We just danced a little bit and Miss Carmen Estrellada wrote some things down. I didn't know what she was doing."

"There were tryouts," I said again.

"No, it wasn't a tryout situation. Fiona, don't feel bad," said Nell. "I'm going to teach you the whole thing. All of it. You'll see."

"What was the party like?" I asked, looking over at the pile of candy Kip was offering Wallace. It was growing by the minute. Wallace was sitting there, watching and waiting, quietly licking a lollipop. A miniature Almond Joy bar is a *very* choice piece of candy. It would take a lot of root-beer barrels and a lot of candy corn to make a fair trade.

"Miss Carmen Estrellada's party was so great," said Nell. "We all had our costumes on and we were waiting in the studio, but we didn't know where Miss Estrellada was. All of a sudden she did a fantastic swan leap and came soaring out of the back room, dressed in a harlequin outfit with a black, lacy mask.

"She spun around, and then she sat down in the middle of the room on the floor with a little Cuban guitar in her arms. It had a painting of a dancer on it."

"Does she play the guitar?" I asked, changing the receiver to my other ear so I could see better what Kip was offering Wallace.

"Yes, she sang us a song in Spanish. It was a Cuban folk song with a story something like 'Sleeping Beauty,' only different," said Nell.

"She sang it in Spanish?" I asked. "How could you understand it?"

"Before she sang it, she told us the story. She translated it. Wanna hear it?" said Nell.

"I'm listening," I said.

"Miss Carmen Estrellada told us the song was about the healing power of dance," said Nell. "This is the way it went. There was once this beautiful villa in the midst of a huge field of sugarcane. But a spell had caused all the happy people who lived and worked in the villa to fall asleep. For years and years everyone there slept, and they couldn't wake up.

"Then one day a harlequin came to town and did a dance in the town square. This dance was magic, and a cat who had been sleeping awoke and started to dance and follow the harlequin. Then the harlequin danced by a baker who slept in his shop, and he awoke and started dancing, too. Soon the harlequin danced around the whole town, and everyone woke up and started dancing and dancing.

"Then Miss Estrellada played the song on the guitar and sang it in Spanish for us. When she was finished she got up and did the harlequin's dance. Afterward she said, 'Dancing heals all wounds. It heals your body and it heals your soul.'" Nell whispered into the phone, "Fiona, it was *so* beautiful."

I looked over and saw Kip putting one more licorice stick on the pile, and the trade was final.

"When are you going to eat this?" said Wallace, handing Kip the Almond Joy.

"I'm not going to eat it," said Kip, closing his eyes and smiling a long, thin, heavenly smile. "I'm going to *save* it."

Wallace collected five licorice sticks, ten root-beer barrels, and ten candy-corn pumpkins in the trade.

"These will come in handy," she said, bagging them up, "when I go for Fiona's Double Bubble gum."

"Wallace, you can *have* my Double Bubble gum," I said into the room, suddenly feeling like I wanted to practice ballet even harder, suddenly feeling like I wanted to get so good, to be *so* light, to almost fly. *That's* how good I want to be.

Now it's six in the morning, and that's when I usually get up to practice ballet. I tiptoe out of my bedroom area, creeping around the dressing screens that act as room dividers. I sneak past the Eleanor Roosevelt couch and the platform rocker covered with embroidered birds. Wallace is sleeping away in her bedroom area behind a pink flowered dressing screen. As I tiptoe by, I look into her room. It's a mess with clothes and bears and books tossed around on the floor. I slip through the double doors.

I have to wear leg warmers, a hat, mittens, two sweaters, and a scarf over my tights and leotard. I close the double doors behind me and walk across the empty, sunny dining room and the bright drawing room. It is very cold out here, and the light is crisp. Through the windows I can see the pink sunrise all along the frozen orchard.

I climb the stairs up to the ballroom, my toe shoes in my arms, swinging from their pink ribbons. In the ballroom the windows have frost on them — feathers and leaves and mountains, a whole world of ice, bathed in pink light. I take two spins in the middle of the room in my practice slippers. Two spins for the morning. Two spins for this great, big, light-filled room. Two spins for Miss Carmen Estrellada's harlequin dance.

I go over to the barre and grab it the way I always do and start warming up. This dance barre is made out of pipes Kip got from the back of his father's truck. They used to be the hot-water pipes that went into Bailey Martin's kitchen.

I lean down to sort through a stack of my father's old, scratchy 78 records. I usually decide on "Blue Moon." On the record jacket a huge blue moon shines over a lake with white hibiscus flowers draped around the border. On the back, a woman sits looking at the blue moon reflected in the water. I put "Blue Moon" on the Victrola. The room is so chilly that the record seems to groan and drag in the cold.

The barre is just the same height as the barre at Nell's dance class, and I work for an hour doing all my positions. Then I go out into the room to do my toes and then my leaps. I go through the whole thing just like Nell does.

Blue moon, you saw me standing alone, without a dream in my heart, without a love of my own. I do first position . . . tendu . . . third position . . . tendu . . . arabesque . . . piqué . . . *Blue moon, you saw me standing alone, without a dream in my heart* . . . fifth position . . . balancé . . . balancé . . . *without a love of my own. Blue moon, you saw me standing alone* . . . first position . . . piqué . . . passé . . . leap . . . leap.

When I run across the room in my toe shoes, I hear the hard tips clacking against the floor, and then I go up on my toes for an arabesque . . . *Blue moon, you saw me standing alone, without a dream in my heart, without a love of my own.* After a while, I get so warm, I start taking off sweaters. There's an old piano in another room down the hall. It's dusty and broken and out of tune, but Wallace and I go in there and try to play it once in a while. Sometimes I can pick out the tune for "Blue Moon." *Blue moon, you saw me standing alone, without a dream in my heart, without a love of my own* . . . fifth position . . . glissade . . . jeté . . . jeté . . . *Blue moon, you knew just what I was there for, you heard me saying a prayer for someone I really could care for.* Most of the records I've found upstairs are old 78s like "Blue Moon." When I put the record on, I usually set the arm on automatic. Then the record plays over and over again. After twenty times or so, I know I'm done. Then all day long "Blue Moon" plays in my head and even though I'm not practicing anymore, I'm thinking about the steps and I'm feeling the music running through me.

My father must have bought that record for my mother when they were young, maybe during the war when he was home on leave. Maybe they walked into a record store and he just bought "Blue Moon" for her on a whim. He was probably wearing his sailor's suit then, and afterward they probably went into one of those photo booths and got a strip of snapshots of the two of them together, before he went back. I've seen the strip of photos from the photo booth in my mother's jewelry box.

Another record I play that belonged to my mother and father from that time is called "I'll Be Home for Christmas." It's sung by a sad-sounding soldier who's saying that he'll be home for Christmas, if only in his dreams. A lot of soldiers heard that song, and then the next day they went out and got shot, my mother told me. But not my father. He didn't get shot then.

After I'm done practicing this morning, I go downstairs and back into our living area. It's warm and dark in here because the huge curtains are drawn, and the woodstove is full of wood and clicks with heat. I get out a dime from my dresser and go to the phone to call Nell. We have a pay phone in our house. It's kind of embarrassing, but that's what we have. If you have a pay phone, then you never have phone bills.

This morning I drop a dime into the phone and I dial Nell's number. Naturally, I get Kenny, her little brother, on the line. He won't give the phone to Nell. He crumples paper into the receiver and then roars into it, and I hear Nell calling to her mother, and then I hear some struggling, and then Nell grabs the phone.

I say, "I was on my toes for almost an hour today."

"Don't push it," says Nell. "You're supposed to do a little each day with toes. Did you get all the steps right?" she asks. Nell is great. I'm sure I'll know every step in the recital very soon. I can hear Kenny crying in the background, and Nell says she has to go.

"See you on Monday," I say. Then I hang up the phone and sit there in the dark warmth of this room, listening to "Blue Moon" playing in my head, over and over again.

CHAPTER X

When I get up to pull the huge curtains back to let in the light, I see something red darting across the yard. It's Kip. He's wearing a red woolen hat that makes me think of a Santa Claus helper's hat, and he's leaping in the air and clapping his feet together (another one of the tricks he works on all the time).

I wave from my window, and then I run out into the dining room, then into the drawing room, then into the hallway, and I open the front door and shout, "Encore! Encore!"

Kip takes a bow. Then he runs toward the house with a paper in his hand. "Look at this," he says. He's been out in the cold and his cheeks are red like his red plaid woolen jacket. "Look at this," he calls again, running and circling the yard with his arms out like an airplane. He zooms and circles and then comes in for a landing at the front door. "What do you think of this?" he says. "A 'Name That Sandwich' contest at Simon's Bakery, and guess what the winning prize is."

"Let's see," I say, pulling on my coat and going outside onto the worn steps, past the two carved marble swans that sit on either side of the front door. "Let's see. How about a guest appearance on *The Mickey Mouse Club*."

"Nope," says Kip, "but you're warm. Keep guessing."

"A child-sized sports car you can really drive around in from FAO Schwarz, preferably red?" Wallace and I spend hours wishing we had that.

"No," says Kip, "but this is just about as good."

"Really?" I say. "Well then, tell me."

"For more details, see me at my house," calls Kip, waving the paper and running off. It's snowing again this morning, a delicate and light snow like angel dust spinning down from the sky. Kip disappears into the small flurry of whiteness.

I follow the path through the woods to his trailer. Kip made this path *entirely* by himself. It runs from the edge of our orchard, through the woods, and right to Kip's front door. He cut the branches and put up little signs that say *Only twenty more yards to see the Kipper and the Furnace Doctor*. A little farther on there's another sign that says *Straight ahead to the Kipton Jones residence*. When you're almost there, you start seeing all these birch trees with a bunch of bark stripped off them, because Kip writes all his letters on birch bark.

When I get up into his little yard, Kip is nowhere to be found. I knock on the metal door to the trailer. Kip's father comes to the door. His hands are stained dark with furnace oil and grease, and no matter how much he washes them, it never really comes out.

Once Kip told us that his father is shy about the way his hands look. "He's stuck with it. What can he do? It's his living," said Kip.

"Well," said Wallace, who was standing there at the time, looking sad, "no problem. He could just put his hands in his pockets!"

Kip's father smiles now and pulls the door open wider. He has a spatula in his hand and a dishcloth hanging from his waist.

"Is Kip here?" I ask.

"He was a minute ago," says Kip's father, and then he shouts, "KIPPER!" out the door. "KIPPER," he shouts up into the woods. "Well, he's here somewhere, so come on in. I'm sure he'll be back in a moment," says Kip's father, stepping away from the door. "You can wait in here if you want."

I walk into the living room, which has brown wood paneling on the walls. There's a wooden wagon-wheel table and wooden chairs with backs that look like wagon wheels.

I've never been over here before without Wallace. Even if I sneak away, she usually figures out where I've gone and comes zooming after me. I expect I'll see her head bobbing at one of the windows any minute now.

I sit down on a couch with stagecoaches and horses printed all over it. The couch slants a little, so you almost feel like you're going to slip into one of the crevices between the cushions.

Kip's father is in the kitchen frying up corned-beef hash for breakfast. It smells delicious and mingles with the sweet, musty smell coming from the couches. Now Kip's father is chopping onions. I can see his tattoo on his upper arm from here. It's a pretty picture of a hummingbird.

I go over to the front door and shout out, "Kip! I'm at your house and I'm waiting for you." Kip wishes he lived in a big, echoey place like ours, and we wish we lived in a trailer like his. It's so warm in here, and in the kitchen everything works.

I walk back through the living room and down the narrow, paneled corridor to Kip's room. Kip has a Davy Crockett lamp on a table near his bed and all sorts of hotel pamphlets pinned on the walls and a huge poster of a building made out of corn-cobs. On the bottom it says *Visit the Corn Palace, Mitchell, South Dakota, a MUST on your trip out West.*

On Kip's desk I see his detective kit in a small box. Above the kit on the wall are a bunch of fingerprints on pieces of paper. He has my fingerprints, my mother's, his dad's, Nell's, and Wallace's.

Kip had to save up twenty box tops of Oaty Oats cereal in order to get the detective kit. By the time he had the box tops saved, he was eating Oaty Oats cereal for breakfast, lunch, and dinner.

When the kit finally arrived, it had a magnifying glass, an ink pad for making fingerprints, a plastic wallet, and a pair of tin handcuffs.

"That's all there is?" said Kip, looking kind of disappointed.

"Maybe they'll send the trench coat and the hat to you later, Kip," said Wallace, patting Kip's arm. "Maybe those are coming in another box."

But the truth is, I don't think detectives wear trench coats and hats. The detectives that came to our house were wearing sweaters and slacks and they looked so ordinary that if you passed them on the street, you'd never notice them.

Kip's father stands in the kitchen doorway with a plate of eggs and corned-beef hash. "Well, when you get ahold of that rascal, you tell him his breakfast is ready," says Kip's father, pushing a big game of solitaire aside and setting the plate down on the wagon-wheel table. Some of the cards splash to the floor and lie on the curly, brown rug.

Kip's father goes over to the little electric organ opposite the TV set and switches it on. It lights up like a dashboard. He turns a few knobs and starts playing "Way down upon the Swanee River."

That organ used to belong to Kip's mom. She played it all the time before she moved to Deerlodge, Montana. Kip told me she left it because she couldn't fit it in the back of her car. She tried and tried and then she just drove off with the organ standing there in the middle of the driveway.

Even with the organ playing pretty loud, I still hear a funny noise at the window and it takes me a minute to realize Kip has tossed a pebble at the glass. Kip's dad looks over at me. "*There he is*," he says, smiling. His eyes are the exact same blue as the Kipper's, the same blue as the chicory that edges the roads and covers the open fields here in the summer.

"I'll go see what he wants," I say to Kip's dad. But I don't think he hears me since he is getting to the part of "Swanee River" where he always goofs up, and he's watching his hands now like a cat watching a bird.

When I open the front door, I see Kip up on the hill directly above the trailer. "Say hey!" he calls, "Say hey, Fiona, come on up!" Then he disappears over one of the rock ledges up there.

I walk around the Furnace Doctor's van and start up the hill after Kip. There's a row of sleeveless white undershirts hanging on a clothesline out here, big ones for Kip's dad and smaller ones for Kip. My father used to wear those same sleeveless undershirts. As I walk by, I touch one of the shirts and it swings there on the line, frozen solid.

"Hey, Kip, your breakfast is ready, and by the way, what's the prize? What's the prize for winning the 'Name That Sandwich' contest?" I call out. I look back down at Kip's trailer. It's silver and I can see the flat, smooth roof from here. Kip says his trailer is like a tuna-fish can on wheels.

When Wallace hears that she says, "Well, Kip, when you go home at night, do you have to use a can opener to get in?" When Wallace thinks she's said something funny, she repeats it over and over again, hoping to get more laughs, but in my opinion that tactic usually backfires.

I see smoke now over the next hill and I think I might even see smoke signals. Kip is working on that. He tried to send a message to Nell last weekend with smoke, but she didn't see it at all, since she was at her aunt's house in Wappingers Falls at the time.

I finally get up to the very top of this ledge. I turn around and call out, "Kipton Jones, where are you?" I turn around again. I can see all across this high cliff. Down below, through the snow, I can see all the long rows of trees in our orchard and our great big house and the tangled grapevines climbing all over everything. Our house looks so gray and boarded up from here, you wouldn't know anyone lived there at all.

"Kipton Jones," I call out again, and suddenly it comes back to me — "Kipton Jones" in an echo, a real echo! I *have* to tell

Wallace. She'll be *so* happy. It's so strange that she hasn't come over.

This spot is the perfect place to take a photograph. My father loved views like this. "What a terrific view!" he used to say, leaning down and snapping a photograph. He tried to get interesting shots of our family. He got one of me when I was playing with a big red-and-blue inflatable ball. He snapped the picture just as I had tossed the ball up in the sky and was holding out my arms and looking up, up, up, waiting to catch it. That's all you see in the picture is me, reaching toward the sky, waiting for something.

I used to help my father develop his photographs in the darkroom. He let me move the pictures from the developer tray into the fixer bath. It was so neat to see a blank white piece of paper slowly become a photograph.

The one I remember seeing developed was a family shot my father took with a timer button. We were all lined up outside in the garden. My father was holding my hand and my mother had Wallace in her arms. The picture developed slowly in the bath, slowly, slowly appearing like a ship in the fog, everything coming in in pale grays and then darkening down . . . my mother, Wallace, me. My father's face was the slowest part to develop.

"Daddy," I said, "Daddy, you're not in the picture."

And he put his hand on my back and said, "Yes, I am, Sweetie. There I am. I'm coming in slower, but I'm right there."

○ ○ ○ ○

I follow a little path over the hill through some scrubby-looking pine trees that seem to be hugging the ground for protection from the wind. The path dips down and then goes back up over another hill and there Kip is. *Finally.*

He's got a campfire going and he has his dinner pail and a thermos of cocoa with him. The fire smokes and spatters and crackles in front of him.

"Hey, Pokey, I thought you would have seen my smoke signals long ago," says Kip, smiling. "I had a great series of three puffs going and I was sure you saw it."

Kip pours a cup of cocoa and hands it to me. In the cold it tastes so delicious and hot, especially with the little stars of snow that keep falling in it.

"Your breakfast is ready, Kip. Your dad cooked it," I say.

"Oh, I have my Oaty Oats right here," Kip says, patting his dinner pail. "Anyway, my dad always eats *his* breakfast and then he ends up eating mine, too. He always eats two breakfasts. He's used to it." Kip says, taking a sip of cocoa.

Behind Kip, I can see way far away, valleys and towns and rivers in the distance. I can even see the Taconic State Parkway, that beautiful, perfect, smooth, double road rolling through the hills.

"Okay, Kip, what's the prize for winning the 'Name That Sandwich' contest?" I say.

"Oh, *that*," he says, beaming. "Oh, I know I'm going to win, Fiona. *I know.* We win things in my family. We just naturally win prizes."

"You do?" I say. "Like what?"

"Oh, like say a few years ago my dad won a shopping spree at Robert Hall clothing store. He had five minutes to run around and throw all these suits in a shopping cart," Kip says.

"Did he get a lot of nice stuff?" I ask.

"Well, he didn't have time to try anything on, so a lot of the suits don't fit him, but he never wears suits anyway."

I start singing the ad for Robert Hall that I hear on my radio all the time, and then Kip joins in. "You see, once you break down the winning barrier," says Kip, leaping to his feet, "then you start winning contests all the time. It's all about the winning barrier."

"What else has your dad won?" I ask.

"Well," says Kip, nodding his head, raising his eyebrows, and smiling, "nothing else *yet,* but we're just getting started!"

I take another sip of warm cocoa. I love the smell of the wood smoke and the sound of the crackling sticks as they burn.

"And I've already got a great idea for a sandwich name," says Kip. "What do you think of the Simple Simon Sandwich, because Simon is the name of the baker there?"

"Gee, I bet that's the winner," I say. "That's really good. You've as good as won, Kip. What's the prize?" I ask again, hoping it will be easier now to get the answer.

Kip looks at me. He's smiling with his whole face. His face has an elfish, beaming look to it, and his eyes are chicory blue and full of light. "The prize is a weekend stay for the whole family at the Biltmore Hotel in Schenectady, New York!"

CHAPTER XI

When it's time to put the fire out, we stomp snow on it and then Kip pours the last of the cocoa over it. As it fizzles and smokes and goes out, Kip says, "I thought of *another* perfect name for a sandwich!" Then he jumps up like a jack-in-the-box. "Yippee!" he shouts, "I've got it! Schenectady, New York, here I come! Come on, Fiona," he says to me, "get on your horse, and let's get out of here."

Kip slings his leg over an invisible saddle, jostles invisible reins, and gallops off on his long legs, calling out, "Giddy up there, horsie!" He whinnies and whines and gallops away down the hill into the woods.

I'm left standing on this high, high ledge with the whole world spread out below me like a Chutes and Ladders game board. I'm still whistling the Robert Hall shopping song, and as I spin around the wind rolls under my coat and puffs it out like a circus tent. If there is such a thing as a summer coat, then this is it. It's blue with blue velvet cuffs, and it used to belong to my cousin, Candy Clark, who I have decided must be quite the party girl. I know there was once a blue velvet hat that went with the coat, because I saw a photograph of Candy Clark wearing it. I never got the hat.

You can learn a lot from studying photographs. Wallace and I spend a lot of time going through a box that ended up being kept hidden away in a built-in cupboard in the huge, empty dining room. We have pictures of our house in Connecticut, where we used to live in the winter. I haven't been able to convince Wallace that we actually ever lived there.

There are photos in that box, too, of my grandmother, who was Elana Rostopola, the Russian ballerina. When she was young, she danced on stages in Paris and Berlin and Madrid. When she came to America, she always stayed at the Waldorf-Astoria, and we would go there to visit her.

My father always wanted to surprise my grandmother, so he would have me step out of the elevator into the hotel lounge in my ballet shoes. He would have the hotel pianist play something, and I would do a little ballet dance. My grandmother always loved it, and she clapped afterward forever.

Then she and my father would murmur together on a couch about my form and my turnout. Then we'd all go into one of the little restaurants off the lobby, and I would always order Waldorf salad.

Kip is wild to know every little thing about the Waldorf-Astoria. He wants to know details I can't tell him, like if the valet parking was exceptional or just up to standard and things like that.

Wallace is willing to give Kip any information he wants about the Waldorf-Astoria (she thinks it's called the Waldorf-Hysteria). She says they deliver a little red sports car (FAO Schwarz) right to your room and you can spend the whole time driving around on the rug. I always roll my eyes when she tells that one.

I still can't figure out why Wallace didn't come over to Kip's house. Usually she's pelting along, catching up with me. That's when I'll say, "Wallace, why can't you let me do anything alone?" And she'll say something like, "What? I just happened to be walking by, that's all."

I turn around now and look at the world below me. Even though it's snowing, I can actually see Kip running through the orchard to our house. He loops through the trees quick as a wink. Oh, it's hard to outfox the Kipper, but I think I might just have done that. This will save me a lot of time.

I take off down the hill, running faster and faster. Then I do a grand jeté and sail over parts of the path.

My grandmother always looked like a ballerina, even when she was old. She always wore her blondish-gray hair in a ballet bun with a pretty silk ribbon tied around it. Her arms were always graceful, her hands two butterflies flitting as she talked. She always had wonderful ribbons in her suitcase, ribbons of every color, some plaid, some with stripes, some with flowers on them. I used to love to sit on the floor and look through the ribbons in her suitcase.

I never saw my grandmother dance, because, of course, she wasn't dancing anymore by the time I was born. But my father had a 16 mm movie projector, and at night sometimes for friends he would put on an old black-and-white movie of Elana Rostopola dancing to sad, beautiful cello music in a fluffy, pale dress with a pale flower in her hair.

The film was old and it was covered with scratches, but I always loved to watch my grandmother dance, and I wanted to dance like her. I wanted to be like her.

"You will be," my father said to me one night after his friends had all gone home. "You look so much like her, and you dance so beautifully for such a little girl." Then he kissed both my cheeks and picked me and Wallace up at the same time and took us up to our beds.

Sometimes my grandmother didn't answer questions with words, she just smiled. My grandmother had a dancer's smile. What is a dancer's smile? It's a smile that is always thinking of grace and balance and form and music. It is a smile of joy.

Even though I can't be a part of Miss Carmen Estrellada's dance class or her Christmas recital, I still have a dancer's smile. And if people can't see it, it is because it is deep down in my heart.

○ ○ ○ ○

When I get back to the house, there's no sign of Kip at all, until I go in the front door. There I find a piece of paper taped to the stair banister with an arrow on it pointing up the stairs. *Find me,* it says in big red letters.

Wallace is standing in the hall. She looks grumpy and messy, like she just woke up.

"Hey, Wallace, how come you didn't come over to Kip's?" I say. "Did he come through here?"

Wallace sits down on a lower step. She has a piggy bank in her hands, and she's trying to shake out the pennies. "My teacher doesn't know about my school project," says Wallace. "It wasn't just *my* project, it was the whole class's project. We worked on it for two weeks." The piggy bank is a glass pig with goofy-looking, shiny eyes that move as Wallace shakes it. "Kip's upstairs," says Wallace, "across the ballroom in the boarded-up wing. He told me."

I step around Wallace and then leap up the stairs, four at a time. When I get up to the landing, I look straight down and see Wallace sitting there on the bottom step with her long yellow braids trailing down her back. "Think of a name for a sandwich, Wallace, and you can win a prize."

She looks up at me, and suddenly she's smiling away.

I hate the boarded-up wing on the other side of the ballroom, because it's so dark and cold there. All the doors you open, open into rooms with heavily curtained or boarded-up windows. Once we found a trunk full of old clothes and hats in one of those rooms. We used them in a special performance of "Swan Lake." (Unfortunately, we had no audience.) We had found a cape of white ostrich feathers in that trunk, which was perfect for the swan, but as the dance progressed the cape fell apart, making it look as if the swan was losing all her feathers. "I think this ballet is called 'The Sick Swan,' " said Kip.

When I'm in this part of the house, I always feel scared, even though I know there's nothing up here . . . not even any furniture, since the antique dealers took all of that away a long time ago.

"Ally ally outs in free-o!" I call out. That's what you say when you're playing hide-and-seek, and isn't that what Kip's playing? Then I add in, "Kippo!" since it sounds good with free-o. I call him Kippo quite often.

His dad always calls him Kipper. He says sometimes, when he's talking to my mother, "Well, I've got to go to work. I've got to put food on the table for the Kipper." Once we heard his dad call him Senator. He said, "It's time for bed, Senator."

Wallace heard that, and she thought it was funny. Now she often says to Kip, "Don't forget your dinner pail, Senator." Or, "You're hogging the couch, Senator. Move over."

I have no idea which door Kip went through. I shiver and push open one at the end of the long hallway. "Ally ally outs in free-o, Kippo!" I call into the room. You'd be amazed how much time I spend looking for Kippo. When he isn't dying, he's hiding on me.

Now I peer into the dark-curtained room before me. It used to be my mother's studio. It's full of statues and draped, dusty sheets. Some of the statues seem to be leaning over thinking of something in the darkness, as if they're listening to music that is too soft for me to hear. One man looks away into the distance, as if he sees something far away that is better than what is right in front of him.

On the floor there are all sorts of hammers and chisels and carving tools flung around. For a long time now our mother hasn't worked in here. It's strange to be walking among all these silent and still people. I'm the only one who can move or speak. "Mr. Know-it-all," I call out, and it echoes in the studio.

I push open the huge curtains that cloak the windows, and the room is instantaneously filled with dazzling white, snowy light. I go over to the window seat and sit down and look out the window. From here I can see the marble angel across the yard in the lower garden. In the snow she appears to be almost flying through the whiteness. She is steady in the rush of snow, watching over the little pond below her.

My father used to say to me when I was little, when I sat on his lap, "If a magical being showed up one day and offered you *one* wish, what would your wish be?"

And I would say something dumb like, "I'd wish for a bride doll." Or, "I'd wish for a new bike."

And then my father would say, "Why wouldn't you make your one wish that *all* your wishes would always come true?"

And I would say, "Yeah, that's a great wish. *That's* the wish I'd wish for."

Now as I sit here in the cold, my breath puffing and billowing white around me, watching the marble angel standing in the swirl of snow in the lower garden, I wish for one thing. Not for every wish to come true, because I know that's not possible. I just want one thing. One. I want to dance in the Christmas recital.

Chapter XII

For the next couple of weeks Wallace continued to act a little bit strange. Her favorite holiday is Thanksgiving, and it wasn't far off. Wallace wasn't drawing her usual pink-and-blue turkeys for place mats. She wasn't going around singing, "Gobble wobble, gobble wobble, feeling fine, gobble wobble, gobble wobble, get in line. Gobble wobble, gobble wobble, what have you got? Kick up your heels and do the turkey trot!" Then Wallace used to go into a made-up turkey trot, shuffling and whistling.

It seemed really odd that she wasn't jumping across the living room, leaping from the Eleanor Roosevelt couch to a chair, to a footstool, to another chair, making it all the way across the room without touching the floor, the way she usually does. And she wasn't coming up with billions of weird ideas for what we ought to make for Thanksgiving dinner. I guess Wallace seemed kind of mopey.

Still it surprised me when Look-Alike Day came along at

school and Wallace hardly seemed to care. On Look-Alike Day we have to dress exactly like a friend.

Nell and I dressed in gray wool skirts with navy blue sweaters. I had a gray skirt that had been my cousin Candy Clark's two years ago, and Nell had an extra navy blue sweater that is her mother's, so I wore that (it was huge). Except for our shoes, we matched exactly. Everyone said we looked like the Bobbsey Twins.

Wallace was supposed to do a look-alike with Shorkey, but he called the night before and said he had a stomachache and wouldn't be going to school.

"Thank goodness he told you, Wallace," I said. "Wouldn't you have felt dumb showing up looking like nobody?"

"Yeah," said Wallace, staring down at her feet. I kind of guessed at the time her class project had something to do with the way she was acting. She told the teacher she'd be bringing it in soon. But how can you bring something in when it's floating down the river, probably passing through Kalamazoo, Michigan, by now?

"I can't be look-alikes with Shorkey, so I guess I can't go to school, either," said Wallace, picking up her piggy bank and shaking it.

"We have to call someone, Wallace. You can't let this happen. Let's get the phone book."

"It's no use," said Wallace. "Everybody already has a look-alike, except for maybe this tiny, shy little kid who has everything in the whole wide world . . . ponies and dogs and everything."

"What's her name?" I asked, picking up the phone book.

"Her name is Wendy Stevens."

"Wallace, I think you should call Wendy," I said. "Let's look up the number."

We looked up Stevens on Evans Street and dialed the number. Her mother answered the phone. She said, "Wendy can't come to the phone. Her daddy is reading her a story right now. After we have dinner and Wendy has her bath and she's in her pajamas all ready for bed, I'll have her call you. Okay?"

"Have her call Wallace Hopper," I said, looking over at Wallace, who was sitting on the floor in her scuffed-up saddle shoes without socks, with her long yellow braids hiding her face.

"Oh, great," said Wallace, sitting down at the kitchen table later, "look-alikes with somebody who's about two feet tall and has everything in the whole wide world."

"Okay, Wallace," I said, "look-alikes with Wendy is better than look-alikes with no one at all."

So when Wendy called Wallace, Wallace started asking her, "Do you have a pink dress with poodles and Eiffel Towers all over it?"

There was a long silence.

"Do you have a red dress with a big, lacy collar and watermelon buttons down the front?"

Another long silence.

"How about a green dress with pompoms and batons and flags all over the skirt and a matching organdy vest?" (Some of the clothes our cousin Candy Clark sent us border on strange.)

There was another long pause. "Wallace," I said, "I have an idea for you. Tell Wendy to meet you tomorrow morning before school."

Then Wallace and I found a long floor-length Hawaiian muumuu that used to be mine, and before that it was, you guessed it, my cousin Candy Clark's. (Our mother says it's a good thing Candy Clark has been such a clotheshorse.) We cut the muumuu off at the knees, and with the remaining part of the material, we added a top and made a tiny muumuu for Wendy.

"She's a shrimp," said Wallace, "so make it small."

Naturally, we weren't professional tailors, but it held together, and we even had enough fabric to make matching bows for Wendy and Wallace. Wallace and I spent hours on the outfit for Wendy. We stayed up till about midnight.

On the school bus this morning, Wallace was kicking the seat in front of her and staring at her Huckleberry Hound lunch box. "Wallace," I said, "just tell your teacher the truth. Just tell her you lost the whole project when the wind blew. Quit lying about it. Quit saying you're going to be bringing it in. You're making everything worse."

Then Wallace opened her lunch box, and we started eating the snowman cake that we had made the night before. It was a yellow-cake mix, baked and shaped to look like a snowman, and then we iced it with marshmallow fluff (Kip's idea).

"Come on, Isabelle Irene," I said as we got off the bus, "just tell the teacher and get it over with."

"Oh, great," said Wallace at school, when Nell and I had finished getting her arranged in her muumuu in the girls' bathroom. Then the three of us stood there with the extra little dress and bow, waiting for Wendy. We waited a long time. We waited and waited and waited.

"Oh, great," said Wallace. "This might be the worst day of my life."

But I thought Wallace looked really cute in her Hawaiian-print muumuu dress. As she went off down the hall with Wendy's little outfit in her arms, Nell called out, "Wallace, maybe Wendy went to the library. Look for her." Wallace walked away very slowly, very slowly, with her arms out as if she were wading into a pool of water.

After Nell and I fixed Wallace's look-alike outfit this morning, we headed down the hall for our classroom. Usually we get a chance to go to the gym to practice, but today we were very late. We had waited for Wendy to show up till all the halls were empty and silent and all the classes had started. Just as we got to our door, Nell paused before turning the knob and said, "There are tryouts today. Because of Wendy, I forgot to tell you. Miss Estrellada is holding tryouts for the recital. One dancer, Janie Trotter, who has the part of the Rose Petal Princess, hurt her ankle ice skating, and she can't dance. It's an open tryout at the studio after school at three-fifteen. You can try out, Fiona."

"What did you say?" I asked.

"You heard me," Nell said, smiling.

The rest of the morning was great. Nell and I won the look-alike wheelbarrow relay race in gym class even though we were giggling the whole time. And Peter Collins cut ahead of us in the lunch line and said, "Great look-alikes. Are you two twins?"

"Yeah," we said, as he cut ahead even farther up the line, "we're the Bobbsey Twins," but he didn't even hear us. Normally it takes almost fifteen minutes to move through the line, but Peter Collins cut in smoothly next to Doreen and Julie and started asking them about a math problem. They're both great at math, and Doreen was once invited to be on *Quiz Bowl* because she adds so fast.

Soon Peter Collins was moving into the cafeteria with a tray of mashed potatoes, hot turkey, and gravy steaming in front of him. He was joking around as he passed various tables of sixth-grade girls. By the time Nell and I moved through the line, Peter Collins had pretty much finished his hot lunch.

I didn't need to be in line, but I wanted to wait with Nell to keep up our Bobbsey Twins impression. I had my Mouseketeer lunch box with me, containing the snowman cake and a cheese sandwich, not our favorite Velveeta cheese, but some strong cheese my mother buys that we don't really like. *In fact,* I thought, *when Wallace goes to open her lunch box, I bet she wads up the sandwich and sends it flying into the trash can. That's what I bet.*

From where Nell and I were sitting we could see Kip on the other side of the room, standing up on his chair doing his french-fry toss. A college guy, who is the lunch-line monitor, went over to tell him to sit down. Soon the college guy was trying the french-fry toss, too.

"Mr. Know-it-all," I said to Nell.

And she went, "Yeah."

Now it's one o'clock, and Nell is beginning to prepare me for the tryouts. "You wear a black leotard and white tights. Here they are," she says, handing me everything. Her eyes are as green as a green crayon.

We are in the hall near the door to the junior high. Through the double doors, big, grown-up kids nudge and push as they change classes.

"Miss Estrellada is expecting you, Fiona, at three-fifteen." Nell says Miss Estrellada's name with a whisper. Through a window in the hall, the junior high swimming pool is visible. A group of teenagers in swimming caps and black tank suits line up for diving class. There is a sound of shouting that echoes in the pool room, and the watery smell of chlorine drifts out to the hallway.

"Don't be late, Fiona. Miss Estrellada hates late more than anything. Meet me at the dance studio at three o'clock sharp. I'll be waiting." Nell waves good-bye to me and I see she has written "Good Luck, Fiona" on the palm of her hand.

At two-fifteen during science class Ronnie J. is at the blackboard writing in white, squeaking chalk, "What is an Insect?" Then he begins a complicated-looking diagram of a June bug, with arrows pointing here and there. Then he spells out words like *membranous wing* and *thorax*. Ronnie J. is really obsessed with bugs. He loves them. As the chalk squeaks away, and he draws every hair on the June bug's antennae, I start going over and over in my mind the steps Nell has taught me for the part of the Rose Petal Princess (Janie Trotter's part).

The recital is called "The Dance of the Winter Moon," and it features various flower princesses that come to life and dance under a full moon on a dark, cold winter night. Nell has the part of the Camellia Princess, and as she dances, someone tosses fake snowflakes from above. It makes Nell nervous, because she's afraid she'll slip since the snow is actually Ivory soap flakes.

Someone else has the part of the Red Peony Princess, and then there is the principal dancer, an older girl named Jasmine, who plays the part of the Spirit of Winter, who tries to dance all the flowers back into sleep until spring. There are about twenty different flower parts, and snow is dusted and tossed, and the moon glows as the flowers dance. At the end, the flowers drift offstage as if they are floating away into the falling snow.

Nell told me the moon is cut from a huge piece of cardboard and then painted a fluorescent bluish white. When the lights are pointed at it, it really looks as if it is shining in the dark sky. The stars are painted, too, in fluorescent paint, and the lighting is dim and focuses just on the moon and the spot where the dancers dance.

As Ronnie J. is beginning a large drawing of a long-horned grasshopper, I am thinking, *Four steps . . . turn . . . arabesque . . . fifth position . . . pas de bourré . . . arabesque.* Miss Estrellada will play the piano and a kid from the high school, who won an award at the music conservatory last summer, will play the violin.

At two-thirty I have butterflies in my stomach. I can't listen to Miss Johnson talk about the Algonquin Indian method of building a canoe. She is just saying that our town name means "little place where the wind stirs" in Algonquin Indian. And it's true —

it's very windy here and even more windy up on the bluff where I live. You can feel the presence of the Algonquin Indians among the woods there, and Kip once found a scoop that Miss Johnson thinks is Algonquin Indian.

Little Place Where the Wind Stirs, our town. Miss Johnson says our town is also in the "snowbelt," which is definitely true. It is snowing now as I look out the window. It is deep and fluffy, and I think, *Kip and I and Wallace will probably build a snow fort when we get home. But that will be very late, since I will be at tryouts.* The word *tryouts* makes the butterflies in my stomach lift and flutter around. I start thinking about my steps again . . . *fourth position . . . jeté . . . arabesque* . . . I am almost shaking, I am so nervous.

At two-forty-five the principal comes to our class and asks Miss Johnson if I can come out to the hallway to talk to him. I have never talked directly to the principal before. Everyone is afraid of him. Going to the principal's office is something Nell or I would *never* have to do. Wallace got sent once when she threw a wad of paper, aiming at the wastebasket, and hit the teacher in the face by mistake. She said the principal was nice to her, though, and let her play with pick-up-sticks while she was at his office.

Now he is standing there with one hand lightly passing over his necktie, and then he leans it against a locker. (It is Bobby Quin's locker, with chewing gum and dents all over it.)

"Fiona Hopper," the principal says, "what was your sister Wallace wearing today in class?"

"An orange-and-purple Hawaiian-print muumuu, an orange-and-purple Hawaiian-print bow in her hair, and a pair of saddle shoes without socks. A lot of times, she doesn't wear socks," I say.

"Did she have a coat?" he asks.

"Yes," I say, "a brown coat." I am wondering why the principal wants to know so much about Wallace's wardrobe. I am almost about to bring up my cousin Candy Clark when the principal says:

"Fiona, your little sister is missing. We figure she's been missing since around eleven this morning. We called your mother, and she's coming down right now. Because of the snowstorm we are having, this is very serious. Fiona, did Wallace have something bothering her, some reason to run away or anything?"

I don't hear anything else the principal is saying. Everything starts to tumble through my head at once . . . the way Wallace hates her name, the lost school project, having to be look-alikes with nobody, the way she misses our father . . . *everything*.

With all this going through my mind, I don't say anything to the principal. I can't even answer him. I just run to the door and go out into the playground and shout, "Wallace!"

I don't have my coat on. It's a blizzard out here. I run past the bushes where we usually play and hide during recess. They are covered in heavy snow. The swing set is stiff with cold, and the swings toss in the wind. There is ice on the slide, and the wind rolls over the soccer field, just as I imagine it rolls over fields of snow in Antarctica or Alaska.

"Wallace!" I call.

A police car with its twirling red light pulls up, and our mother gets out. Her face is white, and her hair blows around in the wind.

"Fiona," she shouts, running toward me, "where could Wallace be? What has happened?"

I run back into the school to get my coat and hat and boots and mittens. I wrap my scarf over my face and run back outside. Kip meets me at the door.

"Kip, Wallace has run away. We have to find her."

"I know," says Kip, "everybody's really worried. If she's outdoors, she'll freeze to death."

Our mother calls from the window of the police cruiser, "Fiona, you and Kip stay close by. Look for her around the school." The cruiser pulls away with its lights flashing. They drive out of the parking lot and head toward Main Street.

Kip and I cut across the soccer field, the snow rushing up against us. "Wallace Hopper! Wallace Hopper!" we call, but the snow and wind roar, and there is no answer. We work our way across the field and down a slope where kids sometimes sled. It's a pretty steep incline and, in the right conditions, great sledding. Now we practically fall down the hill. The snow is knee-deep and fluffy, and the wind is persistent.

At the bottom of the hill, we think we find tracks. Kid tracks. Maybe saddle-shoe tracks that go over a second hill and then suddenly are lost in the field of snow. You can't tell where the field stops and where the sky begins. It's all a sea of whiteness.

The same footprints seem to reappear again at the edge of the field near the railroad trestle over the river. The trestle is a shortcut to town. It's dangerous to cross it, because if you're on it when a train comes, there's nowhere to jump, except down into the icy, choppy water below. Later in the winter, this river will be frozen over, but now it's still moving along in a gray torrent.

I look up at the trestle and then down into the dark river. Kip puts his woolly, mittened hand on my back and pats my shoulder. "Don't worry," he says, "we'll find her." Then I follow Kip over the snowy, rickety trestle, knowing Wallace would probably cross this way to save time.

We inch slowly across the railroad tracks on the trestle. They are slippery and wet with snow, and down below the gray water rushes along, churning with the current. I hold on to the wooden railings of the trestle and I think I can hear the whining cry of the three o'clock train not far off.

Kip says, "Hurry, I hear the train whistle!"

I can hear the train now, chugging over the hill beyond, three pulls on the whistle for three o'clock. Kip and I slip and slide over the tracks. I can tell the train isn't far away, because the tracks are trembling a little under my feet. We're halfway across the trestle when I look up and see the enormous, steely face of the engine coming at us on the other side of the river, dredged in steam and smoke. The wheels thunder and then screech as the engineer tries to put on the brakes. I can hear myself screaming and then I feel Kip pulling me over toward the edge of the track, where there's a little ladder that goes down the side of the trestle.

"Hurry, Fiona, go down," he shouts. "I'll follow."

I grab on to the icy ladder rungs and climb down. Kip pushes on behind me just as the train barrels across the trestle, the whistle blowing, the tracks shaking. I get to the bottom of the ladder and there's a little platform tucked under the bridge with the gray, thundering water far below. I climb onto the platform, curl up, and put my head on my knees because I'm trembling so much. The train roars above us and the water roars below us.

"How did you know this was here, Kip?" I shout.

And he shouts back, "Stick with me, Fiona. I know things."

It's a short train, maybe twelve cars rumbling overhead. As the train leaves the trestle, we climb up the ladder and watch it circling through the woods on the other side of the river. There are three cars near the end that say *The Burlington Zephyr* on them.

With the train whistling and puffing in the distance, Kip and I inch across the rest of the trestle and leap off onto the opposite bank of the river. As we climb through the deep snow, Kip reaches down and pulls back a cluster of bushes.

"Look," he says. There among the branches along the river is a group of threads, orange and purple threads from the hem of a Hawaiian muumuu.

I look out into the cold, rushing river that keeps on going no matter what happens. I see a dark form upstream. It looks like an arm reaching out of the water.

"Kip, look!" I shout. "Is that her? Is that Wallace? WALLACE!"

We try to run upstream along the snowy edge of the river. I stumble on a slippery rock underneath the snow and fall down the bank, but I grab a small bush and stop myself from sliding into the water.

"Wallace," I call upstream, "Wallace, *please* answer!"

Kip gets up there first, looking out into the water, with the snow blowing around his legs and the wind pulling on him, dragging on his clothes.

"Is it Wallace? Tell me right now, Kip!" I scream.

Kip stands there a second, squinting into the water. "No, Fiona. It's just a branch. It's not Wallace," he says.

○ ○ ○ ○

Kip wades all the way across another field of snow and into a small woods, and I follow him, stepping in his footprints like in the Christmas song "Good King Wenceslas." Then the woods break off short, and we're on an old asphalt parking lot where there used to be a drive-in movie theater. The metal posts that used to hold the speakers stick up out of the snow. A big rusty sign says *Welcome to Wegee Movie Land, speed limit five miles an hour.*

We cross Wegee Movie Land and head toward Main Street, coming at it from behind. We see only the backs of stores, windows filled with old things, like cardboard packing materials and last year's poster of an ad for Philip Morris cigarettes. Wallace likes that ad, because there's a bellhop in it standing inside a fancy hotel. It says *Call for Philip Morris.*

We scramble up an icy alley and turn the corner and walk into the newspaper-and-candy store. Marty Pippin is behind the counter reading a paper. The air is sweet with the smell of pipe tobacco. It's nice and warm in here, but my cheeks still feel numb from the cold.

Kip knows Marty Pippin. I don't. Marty Pippin is a friend of Kip's dad. They go fishing on Saturdays, and sometimes they go to the Knights of Columbus hall together. (Kip's been in there and says it has absolutely nothing to do with King Arthur or any knights at all.)

Now Kip stomps the snow off his boots on the doormat. And Marty Pippin says, "Snowing enough for you, Kipper?"

And Kip goes, "Sheesh! I guess so."

"Your old man still working out at the subdivision, or is that job past history already?"

"Oh, he's still working out there. They are trying to get it done by Christmas," says Kip. "Marty, have you seen a little kid in here?"

"What?" Marty says. "Kids are in here all the time. Sure, I've seen a little kid, which one?"

"A Wallace kid," I say. "She has long, blonde braids and red cheeks. She wears saddle shoes with no socks, and she's a little bit messy-looking."

"Well, there was a little girl in here this morning. I asked her why she wasn't in school, and she told me what sounded like a tall tale. She had a piggy bank with her, and she wanted to buy some candy, but she couldn't get the money out. She disappeared while I was in the back room bringing up the out-of-town papers."

"She's lost," I say, and I start to cry. Then I hear the siren on the police cruiser wailing as it climbs the hill beyond the stores in town.

When Kip and I leave the store, it's about four in the afternoon, and the sun burns pink in the sky against the snow. Just as I look up at the hill covered in houses above the town and the snow drifting against the pink sky, I remember the dance auditions — the tryouts at Miss Estrellada's dance studio at three-fifteen. They're over. I missed my chance.

At five o'clock, another cruiser sets out and radio stations are alerted because of the storm.

"We wouldn't be so concerned," says a traffic cop on the corner, "if your sister had wandered off on a beautiful day, but weather like this is dangerous."

"She hates her name," I tell the traffic cop, "and she lost a big school project, but it wasn't her fault."

Darkness settles in now, and houses have their lights on. I shiver as we walk up the hill past the library.

"Come on," says Kip, "let's check in here. She could be in here reading or something."

We push open the big, oak, swinging door and trudge in on the shiny, dark tiles of the library foyer, leaving wet footprints behind us. As we walk in, Kip says, "Fiona, think, think. Where would Wallace go?"

"To Seattle," I say, "but she'd never get there."

The library is warm and has a murmuring silence about it that normally is comforting, but tonight it makes me feel anxious. We hurry to the front desk to talk to Mrs. Taft, the head librarian.

Mrs. Taft only knows kids by the books they read. She doesn't know anyone's name. So we say, "Mrs. Taft, have you seen the girl who reads *The Borrowers Afloat* over and over again?"

Mrs. Taft shakes her head. "Is that the little girl who's missing? No, she hasn't been in here tonight." She looks sadly out the window. "My husband is on the search team. Don't worry. They'll find her."

"Let's get going," I whisper. "It's getting dark, and I'm scared."

Outside, the lights of the houses along the hill are soft and velvety, glowing orange in the snow. The storm has stopped, and suddenly the night is crisp and clean and quiet. Even the stars have come out, a million billion of them blinking from a million billion miles away. My teacher, Miss Johnson, says that some of those stars aren't even there anymore, their light took so long to get here. It's so hard to understand or comprehend the distance. Perhaps it's the way a tiny bug looking up at a huge room would feel, unable to even understand what he is somehow a part of.

As we climb the hill, passing houses on Randolph Street, a cold-looking cat scurries away into someone's bushes. And I start remembering how Wallace always gets into the photographs in the built-in cupboard in the dining room, pulls out a framed one of our father, and starts hugging it.

"Wallace," I told her the last time, "you can't hug a photograph. It's only paper. It's no use."

"No, it's not," she said. "It just *looks* like paper, but it's not."

"Wallace Hopper, where are you?" I shout out into the black, quiet, velvety sky.

We pass a plain, white, wooden church with a tall tower and a sharp, white spire that seems to point up to the moon. Kip pulls me by the arm. "Come on," he says, "I have an idea." The church door is open, and we go into the hallway. We even peer into the chapel and see the wooden pews and a large, wooden Madonna standing along the wall. It almost reminds me of my mother's statues. "Come on," says Kip, pulling me back.

We open a little, white door and go up some blue, wooden stairs, past the second floor, through another small door, and up the narrow stairs of the bell tower. Kip seems to know which door is right and where the light switches are.

"I've been here before with my dad when the church furnace broke down last fall," he says. "While my Dad was working, I did a little exploring."

"Kip," I say, "what are we doing? Wallace wouldn't be up here."

"We don't know where she is," says Kip. "From up here we can see the whole landscape, even though it's dark. We'll be able to scope out the situation. Come on."

We climb the narrow and steep steps, around and up, around and up. Finally, we walk through a tiny, arched door with a big latch, and we're outdoors in the top of the bell tower. A big bell hangs on ropes in the center. In plain air from every angle through an arch we have an entire view of the town below, twinkling and glowing and breathing in the heavy, fresh, new snow.

"This is scary," I say, and I creep to the arched opening to look out and down. We can see everything from here, the big, lighted reindeer at Ralph's Red and White, the Christmas lights draped over the streets and along the shops. I can even see my school, and police cars with their spinning lights clustered in the parking lot. Out near the edge of town, I can see a big, blinking-eyed snowplow that almost looks like a toy pushing through the snow.

Kip leans on the ledge and looks out. "If my mother were here," he says, "she'd know where Wallace is, because she's half-Indian, and Indians always know things like that."

"Why do stars twinkle?" I ask, and Kip looks out at the sky for a while, and then he pushes his scarf back over his shoulder and doesn't say anything.

I put my snowy mitten over my eyes. I'm thinking that if Wallace doesn't come home, I won't have anyone to play kickball with in the ballroom at night and no one to jump rope with. And on summer nights, I'll have no one to run through the orchard with, no one to climb way to the top of one of the apple trees with and sing at the top of our lungs at ten o'clock at night, "I Want a Hippopotamus for Christmas." And if Wallace doesn't come home, I'll have no one who will listen with such admiration, her whole face beaming, when I recite my favorite poem, "The Swing," by Robert Louis Stevenson.

Wallace and I are both big swingers. I mean we love to ride high in a swing. We have an old, canvas hammock down in the orchard, and we spend a lot of time out there. You can flop down in that hammock, swing back and forth, eat an apple, and say a poem while you're looking up at the sky.

Wallace loves swinging so much that Mrs. Braverman had Mr. Braverman put up a wooden swing in their backyard, and they don't even have any children or grandchildren.

"Wallace has a great swing at Mrs. Braverman's house," I say to Kip out of the blue, sort of. And then just as I say, "Mrs. Braverman," Kip and I look at each other, and in a snap of a second we both shout, "*Mrs. Braverman!*"

Then Kip jumps up and down, until the bell tower seems to shake and tremble. We run down the narrow stairs, around and down, around and down. Kip shuts off the lights, and we leave, running out into the soft, silent snow.

This was a very big snowstorm, even for being in the snowbelt. Most of the roads are closed until the plows get around, so Kip and I walk up the hill to Mrs. Braverman's house right in the middle of the road.

How quiet everything is with this heavy, new snow muffling all noises, dissolving all roads and boundaries, bringing houses closer together, bringing everything closer together. Even our words seem to leave our mouths and hover close by in the silence.

When we get to the top of the hill, I look up at Mrs. Braverman's house, and my heart sinks, because it's all dark. There's not even a light on, on the front porch, and the shades are not drawn, so as we approach, we can look into Mrs. Braverman's empty, dark living room. Kip and I shake the snow off our boots on the porch and knock on the door. "Mrs. Braverman," we call out, "have you seen Wallace Hopper?" The words have no echo and seem not to go very far.

Kip turns the doorknob, and the door creaks slowly open. "Mrs. Braverman?" says Kip. "Hello? We're looking for Wallace Hopper."

I follow Kip into the warm, dark house. With all the windows unshaded, there is an airy, spacious quality, as if the room were part of the night sky outside. We walk through the living room, the dining room. All is silent here, and waiting. We walk into the kitchen, which smells slightly of cooking gas, like my grandmother's kitchen used to smell. On the refrigerator, in the dim light from the street outside, I can see an old and yellowed newspaper clipping. It's a photograph that shows a man holding up a huge, big fish, and the caption reads *Jed Braverman gets his northern pike and then some.*

We walk into the hall and climb the large, winding stairs at the front of the house. Kip is whispering now. "Mrs. Braverman, I hope you don't mind. We were wondering where Wallace Hopper is?"

At the top of the stairs to the right, a bedroom door is ajar. A radio is on in the bedroom, and we can hear it playing in there in the darkness. A man is singing *Oh, Shenandoah, I long to hear you. Away, you rolling river. Oh, Shenandoah, I long to hear you. Away, I'm bound away, across the wide Missouri.*

"Mrs. Braverman?" Kip calls softly. We walk into the room passing a big, fluffy, round bed with silky pillows all over it. I've only seen round beds in movies, usually in fancy hotels. In the darkness now I can see floating, white curtains covering all the windows. Kip opens a closet. Coats and dresses hang in there in the darkness, motionless and silent. *Oh Shenandoah, I long to hear you. Away, you rolling river. Oh Shenandoah, I long to hear you. Away, I'm bound away, across the wide Missouri.*

We leave the bedroom and walk down the long hallway past closed doors. We turn a corner toward the atrium where Wallace took us on Halloween night.

As we get to the double doors, we see a sliver of light coming from underneath. We open the door and the large, screened inner door and quickly slip in. Most of the birds are singing and dipping and flying about in the atrium, because the lights are on. There is a warm, moist, greenhouse feel to the room, and there is the sound of a fountain bubbling. A parrot squawks and other birds call and chirp.

"Wallace?" I say out loud. "Wallace, are you here?"

We walk around a small palm tree and a huge potted fern, and *there* is Wallace, sitting on the slate floor in her purple-and-orange Hawaiian muumuu, with a parrot perched on her wrist.

"WALLACE!" I say. "Wallace, thank goodness you're here. Do you know how worried we've been?"

Wallace doesn't answer.

"I told your teacher. Everybody knows about the school project, Wallace. Nobody cares. They'd rather have you, Wallace, than a bunch of graphs. You're worth more than a bunch of graphs, Wallace."

There's a new teddy bear with a red bow lying on the floor next to Wallace, with a card tucked under its chin.

"Is this yours?" I ask. "May I read the card?"

Wallace nods and feeds Patsy a piece of tangerine.

The card, which is written with a very shaky hand, says:

Wallace, I bought this for you when I was at Best and Company earlier this month. It's a Christmas present, but I can't wrap it now, since I'm going to the hospital. I was hoping you could help Mr. Braverman take care of our birds, especially Patsy, since Mr. Braverman will probably be a little upset.

Wallace, I also want you to know I really like your name a lot. It's charming, and you wouldn't be Wallace without it.

Love from your friend,
Mrs. Braverman

CHAPTER XIII

When Wallace and Kip and I step out onto Mrs. Braverman's porch, the whole front yard is flickering from the blue-and-red flashing light on a police cruiser. My mother jumps out of the cruiser and pulls Wallace into her arms.

I can't tell if Wallace is still sad or not, because her face is stuffed against my mother's coat. I can't see much of her at all, just her arm, which is locked around her new teddy bear with its staring, yellow eyes and its plain, happy face.

My mother is wearing a great, big coat I don't recognize. It says *Canine Unit* on the sleeve and it has a hood with fur around it. All I can see is my mother's face inside the hood, white and stark like a crying moon.

I go over and hug my mother and my little sister both at the same time. I'm thinking that at least we have each other. I don't say that, though. Instead I just say, "Hey, Wallace, did you see the dog? This is a Canine Unit, Wallace. The dog's name is Alto, and the one back at the station is named Baritone. They gave

Alto your scarf to sniff, Wallace, and then he was supposed to sniff around and find you. But we found you first."

"And we didn't even have a dog!" shouts Kip.

Wallace doesn't answer. She doesn't even notice Alto sitting obediently in a little caged area in the back of the cruiser.

After a while, all the hugging and stuff makes Kip embarrassed, so he starts throwing snowballs at a stop sign. He hits the S first, then the T. By the time he gets to the O, his father has pulled up behind us in the Furnace Doctor's van. Kip runs over and hops in.

We get in the police cruiser and lead the way out of town, followed by Kip and his father. I can hear the chains on the tires slapping against the underside of the car. The snow is so deep and sparkly in the moonlight. It feels like the land of snow where the little girl in the story "The Child of Snow" had to go. Her mother and father had been turned into ice, and she had to bring back a magic flame from the country of snow to warm them. It feels like that land now, with the roofs of houses deep in drifts.

Wallace is sitting quietly next to me. She isn't even kicking the back of the driver's seat like she usually does. She's just hanging on to her big, new teddy bear and looking at her thumbnail, which has peeling nail polish on it.

In the front seat our mother has her face in her hands. Then she lifts her head and turns around to look at Wallace.

"I've been thinking, Wallace," she says. "I've been thinking and thinking." Then she pauses for a long moment and adds, "I've decided I'm going to let you change your name. We can go to the lawyer's office this week. We'll make it official. Any name you want, Wallace. It's all right with me."

Wallace stretches her neck so that she can see out the window. She turns her head toward the land of snow and ice. She looks at the moonlight falling across the long, white fields and at the sprawling, blue shadows of trees on the snow. Wallace looks out the window for a long time.

After a while, she turns around toward us and says quietly, "No, I don't think so. I've changed my mind. I'm going to stay Wallace, after all."

When I look out the back window, I can see Kip leaping around in the front seat of the van, signaling to me. He has this complicated secret sign language that he's always explaining to us. But right now I can't remember what patting the top of your head with your left hand while rubbing the end of your nose with your right hand means.

Wallace's eyes are rolled over toward Kip in the van behind us. She gets up on her knees and looks out the back.

"Wallace," I say, "Kip's doing that secret language, but I forget what two left hand pats on your head means."

"Oh, I know," says Wallace. "He's saying, 'Up ahead the snow is deep. It's a good thing we have chains on our tires.'"

Wallace flips around and slides back in her seat.

"How did you know that, Wallace?" I say.

"Kip's language takes a little guesswork," says Wallace, feeding Alto a lint-covered piece of candy from her pocket. Wallace seems a lot more cheerful now. I can tell by the way she's looking around that she really likes riding in this cruiser. I know she thinks Officer Wolf McKane looks a lot like Mr. Greenjeans.

Another thing I know is Kip would give anything to be riding in this cruiser. (He got to ride in one with his father last year in the Memorial Day parade.) I know he would love this dashboard with all the blinking lights and the little radio that Officer Wolf McKane used to call in to say, "We've got her. Wallace Hopper has been found. I repeat, Wallace Hopper has been found and is in good condition."

Wallace looks cheerful, but sleepy. I can see her eyes closing and her head leaning to one side. It takes a long time to drive through the snow. Now my mother is quietly talking in the front with Officer Wolf McKane.

Kip and Wallace both love riding in a police car. Not me. If it was my choice I'd say, "See you later, alligator." Yup, I'd have to agree with Wallace tonight. I'd rather be in Seattle.

○○○○

We have finally made it home, but we ended up having to walk in the dark up the last part of the hill. Even with the chains on the tires, the cruiser couldn't get through the snow. Officer Wolf McKane carried Wallace, because she fell asleep in the car. My mother held the big police flashlight, and I had to carry the new teddy bear. It kind of felt good to hug something. It wasn't a long walk, and Alto got to run around ahead of us sniffing everything.

When we got up to the front door, we had to push the snow aside to get in. Officer Wolf McKane said, "Gee, I haven't been here in a long time. What's it been, four years?" He put Wallace down in the hallway and stomped the snow off his boots. Wallace didn't know where she was when she opened her eyes.

"You fell asleep, Wallace," I said.

"I did not," she said. "I was faking."

Officer Wolf McKane stands now in the hallway and looks around. He glances into the empty rooms behind me. I feel like covering the doorway with my body. *Stop. Don't look at our house,* I want to say. *Go away.* Then he slaps his gloved hands together and says, "Well, I guess if everything's all right now, I'll round up Alto and be on my way."

It's not that I don't like Officer Wolf McKane. He has a nice face, but it reminds me of things. When I look at his face, it's the way I feel when I'm late for school, or the way I feel when I look out the window at the lonely orchard in the night. Nell thinks

Officer Wolf McKane is handsome. Whenever she mentions his name, I always change the subject.

"Don't look so glum, Fiona," Officer Wolf McKane says to me. "We got your little sister home safe." He pats me on the back. I can feel the wool of his uniform brushing against my arm, and I remember the itchy, rough texture. I have this feeling he's going to say more, and I don't want him to. I want him to not say anything. I wish I could put my hands over my ears. I want to shout out, *NO, NO. Don't say anything else.*

My mother is looking at him, nodding her head up and down, but her eyebrows are pointed up as if she is pleading with Officer McKane. Her head goes up and down, up and down.

Suddenly I can't hear what he's saying anymore. I'm just remembering that I was outside in the garden with Wallace. I was standing near the window of the dining room and I could hear my father and a man I didn't know talking loudly. The man's voice grew louder and louder. He was shouting about money. Then my father started to shout, too. I was right near the window, trying to get a ball that had fallen into a bed of flowers. I was leaning over when I heard the terrible sound, the loudest sound I've ever heard, a terrifying explosion.

Then I heard my mother screaming. It filled the whole valley below. It filled the orchard and the trees along the road. It filled the whole world.

Then the man was running. He was knocking things over. He bumped into me, and I fell in the flowers. Wallace was three and a half, and started to cry. I knew something was wrong, but I didn't want to go into the house.

"Daddy, Daddy," I called out. "Daddy, Daddy, Daddy."

Then I just lay there on my back, with Wallace lost in the tall sunflowers nearby. I just lay there on my back with bees flying all around me and the sky a dreadful, bright blue.

My father was an art dealer. The man was an art collector. He was crazy. He shouted and shouted. Then he shot and killed my daddy while Wallace and I were in the garden. Officer Wolf McKane came to help. He wouldn't let me see my father, and he held me down. I was screaming, "Daddy, Daddy, Daddy."

Chapter XIV

WaLLace and I stand at the window and watch Officer Wolf McKane disappearing down the snowy road, headed back to his cruiser. We can hear Alto yelping, and we can see the flashlight blinking and sweeping through the trees.

Just before Officer Wolf McKane left the house, Wallace had been swinging on his arms and standing on his big police boots. He pulled a dollar bill out of her ear a couple of times, pretended to steal her nose, and gave her a quarter when he said good-bye. Now Wallace keeps standing at the window waving, even though Officer Wolf McKane can't see her, even when I tell her it's time for dinner. I think our mother is cooking chicken noodle soup and making grilled-cheese sandwiches tonight.

"Wallace," I say, "let's go eat dinner. Aren't you hungry? What did you eat when you were lost?"

Finally she starts hopping on one foot through the drawing room and the dining room. She hops on one foot all the way to our living area. Then she pushes through the double doors and drops into a chair on the other side.

"Wallace," I say, "what are you doing?"

"I'm in training," says Wallace, huffing and puffing, catching her breath. "I want to be in the circus when I grow up. I want to be the girl who wears a sequined dress and rides a horse around the ring standing on one leg. This is how you practice."

At the kitchen table our mother is dishing out bowls of chicken noodle soup. She's wearing an apron with teapots and teacups all over it. Her eyes are still swollen from all the crying, but she looks softer and calmer now.

"Dish me up last," says Wallace.

With chicken noodle soup, it's safer to go last. The first person usually ends up with mostly broth. The last person gets all the noodles. I let Wallace go last without protesting tonight. She seems to be back to her old self, up to her usual tricks again. When she gets her soup, she adds a heaping teaspoon of sugar and a big pinch of pepper to it.

"Spicy and sweet," says Wallace, "just the way I like it."

I pretend to eat, stirring my soup and taking tiny sips, but I'm not really hungry. I feel like I have a huge rock in my stomach. No, maybe it's a boulder.

Before dinner is over, I leave Wallace and my mother in the kitchen. I grab my book bag, put on my coat and scarf, and go out into the empty part of the house. Everything is dark and cold here, and the moon is so bright it casts a shadow of me as I walk into the sitting room with the pink marble fireplace and the two pink lions holding up the mantel. I sit down on the floor near the fireplace, and I get out my toe shoes. I look at the long, silk ribbons that I have sewed and resewed so many times. In the cruiser tonight I planned to throw these shoes in the woodstove when I got home. I put them on now, trying to decide.

Then I think about walking to dance class with my father. He was holding my hand. My daddy had really big hands, bigger than an octave on a piano. He was always teaching me things like about octaves and blue moons and how to count to twenty. He's the one who showed me how to tie my shoes. Learning to tie your shoes is a really big deal to a kid. When you learn, it's a very special time, almost like a birthday.

I'm the one who showed Wallace. She was pretty old when I realized no one had taught her. After that, she didn't have these long strings trailing after her everywhere she went. After you can tie your own shoes, you don't look sad and neglected anymore. You look neat and like someone is taking care of you. . . . And that someone is yourself.

When my father walked me to dance class, he always had that camera swinging at his neck. He took lots of pictures of me when I danced. I can remember walking along with him, the way the sidewalk was all worn down and smooth along the curb and how it had bright-green grass growing up between each section. I liked walking to ballet class with my father, especially in the spring when pink bushes were in bloom and it was warm. I can still remember the brick steps up the hill to the dance class in Connecticut, where we used to live. I can remember the big room with the shiny, wood floor where I took dance lessons.

I was about four or five then. At first I was with real little kids. I mean the kind that won't do anything you tell them to do. Soon I got moved ahead and was practicing at the barre with these great, big, tall girls that could leap really high. One girl had a leotard with zebra stripes on it, and she whinnied like a horse when she spun in the air. I was a lot younger, so I wasn't friends with these big, tall girls, but I could always do everything they did and more. And my father was always there on the side. Whenever I saw him there, I always tried my very best, because I liked to make my daddy smile.

I remember how he used to tell my grandmother on the phone, "Mom, she's good. My God, she's going to be as good as you were."

I must have been good. Why else would they have printed a photograph of me with an article in the newspaper about my dance class? I still have the article, but it's yellow and old-looking. I keep it under the velvet padding at the bottom of my jewelry box, so I don't have to see it every time I open the box.

Every day now I practice on my own, and every day that I get better, I think about my father and how he sat smiling at me on the sidelines. Every day I think, *If I just practice hard enough, I can get closer to him, closer to him sitting there smiling at me.*

I reach down and tie the ribbons around my ankles and then I get up en pointe and do a series of small steps across the floor to the window, but my feet seem to drag. It feels as if I can barely move. All the lightness I have worked to put into my feet has disappeared. I missed the dance tryouts. I let my father down. I start to cry.

Then I look out over the orchard, which is hazy in the cold, and I see the huge, soft, glowing moon.

What is a blue moon? Is it real? I used to have the idea that a blue moon was a magical kind of thing, that when a real blue moon shone on you, you could be transformed. If you had been asleep for a long time, a blue moon could wake you, or maybe if you were sick, a blue moon could heal you. Those are the things I thought when I was a little kid when I heard that song.

"Blue moon, you saw me standing alone, without a dream in my heart, without a love of my own . . . blue moon," I whistle to myself to keep from crying, as I stand here looking out the window. Then I slide down to the floor and lean my head against a marble statue of a lion holding up a column between the two rooms. I'm very sleepy. It was so hard looking for Wallace in the storm. Even though it's cold out here, I can feel myself falling asleep. It feels as if I could just sleep forever.

○ ○ ○ ○

When I jolt awake, I can't figure out where I am. How long was I asleep? Why am I on the floor with my ballet shoes on? I hear a really loud thumping sound on the ceiling above me, a loud rapping, a repeated knocking noise. It sounds like someone is trying to break in to the house. Would someone break in so late, in all this cold, when there's nothing in here to steal?

I slip off my toe shoes, button up my coat, and go softly up the wide, dark, winding staircase. I keep hearing that noise. It sounds like someone is breaking out of a locked room.

I climb the stairs slowly and then go around the corner into the ballroom. It's dark and through the large windows I can still see the huge, glowing moon wrapped in a soft haze. Is it my imagination, or does it seem to have a definite blueness to it, a deep, ocean blue, sailing through veils of clouds? The noise stops suddenly, and I think that maybe it was just a tree knocking against the windows up here.

I stand in the center of the dark room and remember how once, last summer when it was our mother's birthday, Kip collected two big jars full of fireflies. He brought them up to the ballroom, turned off all the lights, shut the doors, and then set all the fireflies free. We called our mother upstairs, covered her eyes, and sat her down in the middle of the room. When she opened her eyes, she was sitting in a chair in the middle of the dark ballroom with all these fireflies twinkling all around her and a record playing, Bing Crosby singing her "Happy Birthday." That was the only other time I've seen my mother cry in these four years, and we couldn't tell that night if it was a happy cry or a sad cry.

Now, across the echoing ballroom, I hear more breaking noises, hammering, crashing. I turn on the light switch, and the old candelabra hanging high at the top of the room lights up, making a crackling noise as the warming bulbs hit the cold air. I hurry across to the other side of the room, a little scared, a little nervous, a little curious. Maybe a raccoon got in through the window that Kip broke last fall. I think I see a shadow in the corner. Is it a raccoon? No, it's only one of Wallace's balled-up sweaters.

I follow the noise, pushing out into the long corridor beyond. All the doors are closed, and it's very dark, but I keep following the noise. I breathe in and hold my breath for a minute as I get to the door to my mother's old studio. There's a light in there. I can see it glowing in the big keyhole.

I turn the handle slowly and open the door just a crack. The woodstove is warming the room in there and my mother is standing by a large block of marble. She's got a chisel and hammer in her hands. She's pounding on the marble in front of her, carving out the beginnings of something. Wallace is standing next to her, holding a dried bouquet of flowers and wearing her dress with the poodles and Eiffel Towers all over it. My mother hammers at the marble, and then she looks over at Wallace, and then she chisels some more. Then she looks back at Wallace. Wallace has a little smile on her face, and she's standing perfectly still, like a living statue.

CHAPTER XV

This morning there is a sifting of snow on my windowsill by my bed. When I open the curtain a crack and peak out, everything is so white and fluffy and crisp in the morning light, it doesn't look real. It looks like a stage set. I can almost see the Child of Snow working her way through the white drifts.

I'm staying in bed this morning. School got canceled today because all the roads are closed. Not just because of the snowstorm, but in the night it warmed up and rained, and then the temperature dropped below zero, and the rain turned to ice. So we had an ice storm, on top of a snowstorm. I'm staying in bed because I didn't practice my ballet this morning. It's the first time in two years I haven't practiced. I'm not going to be practicing ever again.

Nell called me at eleven-thirty last night to tell me that Alison Elkhart got the part of the Rose Petal Princess. Nell was all upset. "Alison Elkhart is too tall to be the Rose Petal Princess. You would have been perfect," she said.

Now this morning I sit up in bed. I open the little music box that my grandmother gave me a long time ago and watch the little dancer spin around and around to the music. *Dance, ballerina, dance.* Around and around she spins.

Alison Elkhart is horse crazy. She has fifty ceramic horses in her room, twenty-two horse posters, one hundred three horse postcards, and at least ten blue ribbons for horseback riding, and now she will be the Rose Petal Princess, even though she's too tall for the part.

I push the heavy curtains farther aside and look way out into the orchard. I can tell that in the night it rained and froze again, because the trees are coated in glass. The branches are thick with clear ice, making them look like delicate glass deer antlers. It's an orchard of snow and glass. Several large trees have snapped under the weight of the ice. As I sit here, I can hear the icy branches clicking together in the wind.

Maybe I'll never get dressed and get up again. Maybe I'll just stay in bed forever. Alison Elkhart gets to be the Rose Petal Princess, and the sky is pearly gray. Outside the whole world is frozen and fragile-looking. Breakable. Everything looks breakable.

In the orchard, Kip's father is standing with my mother in the deep snow. I'm surprised to see my mother out there helping. They are pulling at a tree that has fallen against the house. Kip's father has a chain saw. He drags on the starter, and it starts buzzing and bucking as he works through the limb. Kip is nearby holding one end of the branch as his father buzzes it. I can see my mother gesturing and talking to him, having to shout over the noise of the saw.

I close the curtain and put my head under my pillow. I lie here trying to cheer myself up. I think of a story I heard at school about Franklin and Eleanor Roosevelt and how when they were young, they couldn't think of a name for their sailboat. They were sitting outside on the lawn before the boat was put in the water, trying to come up with a name. Then a little, yellow bird called a vireo flew around and around them and landed on the prow. At that moment Franklin and Eleanor both knew that their sailboat should be called the *Vireo*.

At noon, I hear my mother walking into the living area with Kip's father. He drops a pile of logs by the stove.

"These are too green to use, except when the fire gets real hot," he says. "But put one on at night, and she'll burn real slowly right through till morning." Kip's father sounds warm and comforting today, the way I imagine a real furnace would sound, humming away somewhere in this house.

"Would you like some tea?" my mother asks. Her voice seems to have more ups and downs in it this morning. It doesn't sound so flat.

And Kip says, "You bet. I'd love some." (I've never known Kip to refuse *any* food.)

And Kip's father says, "No, thanks. I've got to go deal with a lot of frozen pipes that have burst in town. Everything's a mess. One place had pipes burst on the third floor, and the ceiling crashed down and ruined the second floor. I'll be back for dinner, Kipper. You hold down the fort."

"I'll stay here," says Kip. "Pick me up when you get home. Don't forget, *Perry Mason* is on tonight at eight."

I can see through the crack in my flimsy wall divider. Kip is warming his hands over the stove and smiling. Kip usually smiles a lot. Now through the window in front, I can see the white van pulling away with the words *The Furnace Doctor* rolling right past the front window.

Kip goes back to the kitchen area with my mother, and I can hear the sound of the teakettle gurgling as it starts to boil. Finally, I get out of bed and put on a pair of jeans with red-checked flannel lining and a brass button at the waist that says *American Bandstand* on it. Nothing Candy Clark's mother ever bought for her daughter was plain, not even a pair of jeans. I also put on a shirt, a sweater, and on my feet, my blue Keds. I don't put my hair in braids. I just let it hang all over the place. "Miss Lady Godiva," my mother usually says when I leave it hanging down. I don't know who that is.

I go out into the living area and slouch on the Eleanor Roosevelt couch. Even the little, yellow vireo couldn't cheer me up this morning. I put my Keds on the edge of the woodstove, and they heat up, and then I start to smell burning rubber, so I move them. If I were an Algonquin Indian girl, I would be outside now, running through the woods with the deer. I would be the kind of Indian girl who only associates with animals: rabbits, birds, deer. My name would probably be She Who Runs Only With Deer. The other members of the tribe would see me running at the edge of a field, and they would say, "There goes She Who Runs Only With Deer. It's too bad she never speaks. She must be upset about something. Perhaps we should call her Silent One."

My mother's wind-up clock on the mantel strikes one gong for the half hour. On the clock door, on the glass, there is a painting of a weeping willow and a man leaning down under it with his head in his hands. Next to the clock is a large stuffed loon. It has glass eyes and real feathers. My father used to collect all sorts of stuffed birds that he found in antique stores. We also have a stuffed pheasant on the bookshelf.

It must be twelve-thirty, because the clock only gonged once. I hear a tapping on our window, and I turn my head and see my friend Nell. Her face takes up one square in the many-paned window panel.

"Nell!" I shout out. "You're not supposed to be here."

"How do you get in?" she calls. "Which one is the door?"

"Nell," I shout, "go back, um, this isn't where I live . . . um . . . I'm just visiting."

Nell keeps on shouting, "Fiona, how do you get in? Where's the door?"

"Never mind, Nell. This is not my house. Go back."

"Fiona," shouts Nell, "it's important. Our dance studio is ruined. The pipes burst on the third floor, and water poured down into the dance studio, and the ceiling collapsed. It's wrecked. Miss Estrellada's studio is ruined."

"What?" I say, and then I point to the door and run through the dining room, the drawing room, and the hallway, and open the huge front door and call out, "Nell, over here. How did you get here, Nell? Everything is covered in ice."

"I walked. I had to. The phone lines are down. I couldn't call. I wanted to talk to you. The studio is ruined. The dance recital is in three weeks. Miss Estrellada says we have to cancel. We have nowhere to have the recital, Fiona. The studio is flooded." Nell starts to whimper as she talks, and her teeth are chattering. "And Kenny, that brat, he ate up my chocolate dancer. The one Miss Estrellada gave me on Halloween. He ate up the whole thing. I was going to save it forever. That's when I said, forget it, I'm leaving, and I came up here." Nell starts to cry.

"Come on in, Nell," I say, forgetting to be embarrassed about our big, broken-down, echoing, empty house.

I stand back away from the door, and Nell walks into the hallway. Her eyes roll around the room. Then she leans down and starts to pull off her long, rubber boots. They are wet and snowy and leave pools of water on the floor shaped like wings.

I try quickly to think of a way to explain this house. In my mind I come up with a story about how I'm just baby-sitting here for the day. But then I see Wallace's saddle shoes flung around in the hallway, her book bag on the floor with her papers strewn all over the place. And I don't know how to explain any of that.

Then suddenly I just say, "Nell. Nell, just tell me. Just say it, right now. If you hate my house, and you don't want to be my friend anymore, say it now. Now, Nell!"

Nell walks seriously beside me in her wet stocking feet, her head moving around and around, like one of those dashboard dogs with the bobbing head on springs that Kip's father has in his van. That dog holds a paper in his mouth that says, in big letters, *Smile awhile.*

"Gee whiz," says Nell. "Sheesh, this is a big place. *This* is where you live? Sheesh." Her eyes gleam, like coal, black and then green. "Geez, if I lived here I wouldn't have to be stuck with Kenny right in my face all the time. It's *so* huge. I can't believe how huge it is. I also can't believe Kenny actually ate my chocolate dancer. Can you? Can you believe he did, when he *knew* I was saving it?"

I look over at Nell sideways. Everything seems to be okay. Nothing seems to be different. We walk into the dining room together, just the way we walk downtown together, talking about stuff. Nothing in particular. As we stand here by the sideboard, I show Nell the dumbwaiter.

"Look at this, Nell," I say. "It's called a dumbwaiter." I open the cupboard door. "There's a little, tiny elevator in here on a rope. It's to send a tea tray up to the second or third floor, I suppose, so a servant doesn't have to carry it up the stairs. Once Kip tried to send Wallace up to the second floor that way, but she got scared. We could hear her crying inside the walls, so he hoisted her back down. Put your boots in there, and we'll send them up. I'll show you how it works."

We set Nell's boots in the dumbwaiter, and I pull on the cords until the boots disappear up the shaft.

"This is for the lady in Room 23 who ordered the black-boot soup," I call up the shaft, and then I say to Nell, "Kip calls our house the Wallace Hotel."

I think Wallace might have been listening to me and Nell at the library door, because as soon as I mention the Wallace Hotel, she comes bursting out of the double doors, climbs the little stepladder, hops up on the sideboard where we like to sing, and does her "Chock Full O' Nuts" number.

"This place is, as Peter Collins says, complete-o neat-o," says Nell. "The only trouble is, where do you sit down and all? I mean do you just sit on the floor?"

"Oh, no," says Wallace, "we have all kinds of chairs and things and toys, and I have all my bears and everything, in *there*."

"We don't actually *live* out here," I say, opening the library double doors to our living area. "We actually live in here." I look over at Nell again. Everything still seems to be okay.

We walk into our living area, which is warm from the wood-stove. We pass the Eleanor Roosevelt couch and the red-brocade platform rocker. (Kip's favorite chair. He loves the way it rocks back so far.) We pass the shelves of books, lots of art books full of beautiful paintings. Standing over lamps and against walls here and there are my mother's large, marble statues. Nell looks for a minute at the stuffed pheasant sitting on a small bookshelf. Its feathers are purple and gold and red and brown, all the colors of autumn.

Nell doesn't say much about the big room. She doesn't even ask (thank goodness) about my mother's greenhouse, which is off to the back, to the left. Kip and my mother are in there now.

We can see their fuzzy forms through the plastic. My mother's been starting a batch of zinnias from seeds this week. Kip always helps her water things.

Wallace and I lead Nell into the kitchen area, and we sit down at the table in there.

"See," says Wallace, "I told you we had chairs."

I open a big can of tomato soup and pour it into a pan. Then I have to stand stirring it so it doesn't burn on the bottom, because the hot plate gets *so* hot. Wallace is always burning stuff and then denying it. "It *isn't* burned," she always says. "Now the food has a great, smoky flavor!"

When the soup is hot, Kip suddenly appears, smiling. "I'll have some," he says. So I pour out four mugs of hot cream of tomato soup. We'll take the mugs of soup upstairs to the ballroom and the soup will keep us warm while we're up there — at least the mugs will keep our hands warm.

When we get upstairs to the ballroom, we sit down on the edge of the little stage to eat our soup.

"We hate our house," says Wallace with a big happy smile, "don't we Fiona? We're embarrassed by it, aren't we?"

Wallace is sitting on Huckleberry Hound, and she is holding the new teddy bear Mrs. Braverman gave her. Wallace has a real thing for dogs, I think. She's always drawing them, and whenever we play house out in the orchard with Kip, Wallace always wants to be the dog. Kip wants to be a Cherokee Indian.

"How can we play house," I always say, "with a Cherokee Indian and a dog? Who's the mother? Who's the father? Where are the kids?"

"Woof, woof," Wallace usually says, and starts sitting up with her tongue hanging out.

"We hate our house, and we don't want kids to see it," says Wallace now, taking a big slurp of tomato soup. Kip is lying on his side on the stage, with his arm propping up his head, awkwardly lifting the soupspoon to his mouth with his left hand.

"Fiona's the best dancer I've ever seen," says Kip. "This is where she practices. See that pipe? That's her dance barre. She works at that barre. I fixed it for her. That pipe used to be the hot-water line to Bailey Martin's kitchen." Kip spoons the soup in and turns his head up and swallows it.

"But, Fiona," says Nell, "this huge room would be perfect for our dance recital. Why didn't you tell me? This stage is just beautiful. I mean, it's big, but not too big, and the room could hold a lot of people. *Please,* Fiona. I've been working for this recital for so long. I've worked so hard."

"Yeah," I say, "*I know.*"

"Is there a way to heat it?" asks Nell, looking around. She has a pencil propped behind her ear, and now she suddenly looks like a manager or an architect. Nell stands up and walks to the back of the ballroom with her hands on her hips.

"Sure is," says Kip, head propped up. "Sure is. There's a good chimney there and a place for a stovepipe. A big woodstove in here would more than do the job."

"And," says Wallace loudly and with great enthusiasm, "there's a piano, too, back in there!" She stands up and then sits back down right on Huckleberry Hound's head. He goes *smoosh* into the floor with his bluish fur and his googly dog's eyes. That poor dog. He has a little, red vest, which Wallace has washed about a zillion times.

"It doesn't need washing, Wallace," I tell her. "It isn't even dirty." I wish Wallace took care of her own clothes the way she takes care of Huckleberry Hound's vest and his checkered pants.

Nell goes up onstage and does a little pirouette. Then she takes three running steps into an arabesque and says, "Oh, this stage is perfect." Then she sits down next to Wallace, who is eating one of the cookies she made three days ago, one of her weird concoctions that includes olives (sugar cookies with nuts and olives). She offers one to Nell, who nibbles at it with minnow bites and then says, "Weird," and puts the cookie down. Our cat, Tuxedo, comes over to sniff it and then walks away. Meanwhile, Wallace has eaten two of them and is smiling away, sitting on her stuffed dog.

"Yeah," says Wallace, "and we could fix this whole room up, too, and bring in chairs for all the people to sit in."

Kip lies on his back and says, "Fiona, we could get my dad to help. We could put up a huge Christmas tree and get a wood-stove in here. It could be really neat."

"We could even mop the floor," says Wallace.

"No, I can't," I say to Nell, "I just can't. It wouldn't be possible."

"Think of Miss Estrellada," says Nell, "the way *she* feels. She came all the way from Cuba. She's all alone in some little town in New York State, some little town on the Hudson River with a weird Indian name. She's all alone with her piano and her dance students. All she cares about is dancing. Fiona, please."

"No," I say, "no."

"Fiona, did you know my mother works in the bank with a neighbor of Miss Estrellada's? The neighbor says she sees her on hot summer nights in her backyard. Miss Estrellada will have music playing, and she dances in the moonlight in her white nightdress, when she thinks the whole world is asleep. It's a sight to behold, the neighbor told my mother."

I look over at my dance barre and at my old Victrola on the floor. I think about all the mornings I've worked and worked, and how hard I wished and waited for something that yesterday slipped away, out of my reach forever. I sit on the floor, and then I lie down on my back and look up at the ceiling, which is huge and cracked and has molded plaster roses and cherubs and draping plaster ribbons making a decorative border that goes around the edge of the whole ceiling. I pretend the ceiling is the floor and that I'm walking on it. It makes me feel dizzy and turned around and confused.

This is the room where my parents had their parties, where a sweet, sad jazz band played music all night, where my mother and father's friends and fans joined them. There were many pretty, velvet fainting couches then under the huge windows, and there were gauzy curtains that blew in the breeze from the orchard outside.

After the "incident" (as Mr. Stamford called it, as everybody around here calls it), those same fainting couches were carried away, lifted up and carried off, the way ants carry off debris, even the way ants carry their own dead, just the way ants scurry around taking things away. Ants.

"No," I say again, "no, I can't."

Chapter XVI

"Kip might be going to Schenectady, New York, to stay at the Biltmore, Nell," I say as we slide in our boots on the icy road down the hill to town. "That is, *if* he wins the 'Name That Sandwich' contest they're having at Simon's Bakery. He hasn't won yet, but he's hoping to win."

"He already has his suitcase packed with three pairs of pants, two shirts, and two sweaters," says Wallace.

"Kip, you don't need two sweaters for one weekend," says Nell.

"What if he gets wet or something?" says Wallace.

"Yeah," says Kip, "or what if I have to make an acceptance speech, and I need to look different from the way I looked when I was on the guided tour?"

"There's even a guided tour?" Wallace yells.

"Quit shouting," says Kip. "Of course there'll be a guided tour. It's a big place with a swimming pool and conference rooms and indoor tennis courts and bellhops . . . the works!"

We're pulling an American Flyer sled behind us. It only can

take three people down a hill, but if we squish we might all four get on, but someone's bound to fall off the back. The road is pretty much pure ice. All around us trees bow over, glistening, covered in ice, making whole lacy worlds of icy undergrowth along the road.

A lot of trees have fallen down, and up ahead there's an electrician's truck parked under a sagging line. There's a man with a cold, red face way up on a pole, leaning out against a big, wide leather belt that is strapped around the pole. He has long, sharp nails on the bottom of his boots that he digs into the side of the pole as he works on the electrical box at the top. He waves to us.

"Hey there, kids, stand back," he shouts.

"School got canceled," Wallace calls up to the man.

We walk way around him, and then we get on our sled. Kip sits at the back with his long legs stretching to the front where he will steer with his feet. Then Nell and I sit in front of him, and Wallace stuffs in between us. We give the sled a shove, and we whiz off down the road going pretty fast. Kip steers into the sand and salt on the road to slow us down, and we sail easily down the long hill toward town.

Everything along the way is covered in snow and ice and sparkles like diamonds, the sky blue as a summer day. I love this ride. The whole valley is a panorama and stretches out to the river beyond. This is the sweeping valley where the Algonquin Indians probably grew their crops, and this hill is, perhaps, where they climbed to see who might be coming to visit along the horizon.

"When you see Miss Estrellada's studio, Fiona, you'll change your mind," says Nell as we sail down the hill. "You'll see how terrible it is. You'll see."

The sled slides along smoothly, crackling over the sand and salt. Halfway down the hill, we all start to sing Nell's favorite song, "Run, Don't Walk, to the Nearest Preacher." Wallace always sings it, "Run, don't walk, to the nearest creature." And then if anyone tries to tell her how it's supposed to go, she denies it and sings it her way even louder.

Next we sing Kip's favorite, the theme song from the *Texas Rangers* TV program. Kip thinks one of the rangers is an Indian, so that's why it's his favorite. As we're singing, Kip starts shooting at the air and sky. "Pow, pow," he goes, and the sled swerves.

At the bottom of the hill, the sled rolls to a long, slow stop. It's amazing what a perfect run we had. No one fell off. We try to paddle the air, as if our arms were oars, trying to get the sled to inch along just a little bit farther.

"Come on. Come on," Kip says. "Row harder."

Finally the sled is really stopped, and we roll out into a snow drift. Kip drags the sled behind a big, knotted elder tree. When we go on downtown, Kip will leave it here near Wendy Stevens's yard. He always does that. It has never been stolen. Once he forgot it when his father picked him up in town, and it stayed there for about two weeks, and still nobody stole it.

Wendy Stevens and about four other real little kids "borrowed" it for an afternoon, and I saw them sledding with it on the old grange hill across the street, where everybody goes sledding on Saturdays. All five of those real little kids fit on just great, and they whizzed down the hill about twenty times.

"Let's have our sandwiches now," says Kip. (Knowing we had them with us, I just guessed he wouldn't be able to wait long.) He knocks the snow off the top of the sled and says, "Anyone can sit on this," and we all pile on, except for Wallace, who wants to sit in the snow.

"It's softer," she says, lying back, looking up at the trees.

Kip opens his dinner pail and hands out four potted-ham sandwiches on Wonder bread. Wallace and I absolutely love Wonder bread. It's squishy and white and perfect. You never see a hole or a bump on a piece of Wonder bread. We never get to have it, because our mother only buys whole-wheat bread. We sit there on the sled, eating our Wonder bread sandwiches that taste so delicious in the cold, wintry air.

"If we had the dance recital at your house, Fiona, we could even get pine boughs and wrap them all around the stairs and make wreaths for all the doors in the ballroom," says Nell.

"It could be like from a magazine," says Kip, "all Christmas-y and stuff. We could put candles on little tables and bowls of candy for people to eat."

"I could be the ticket taker," says Wallace. "Come on, Fiona."

Walking down into town, we see more low-slung wires covered in ice, and the big oak tree in front of Marty Pippin's newspaper-and-candy store has snapped in two. A team of men are chain-sawing pieces of it and tossing them into the back of a truck.

We pass the bakery, which seems to be fine, except that there are empty cake stands in the window, and I don't see lines of frosted cookies and circles of red and pink bonbons in boxes. Nell pushes open the door next to the bakery that says *Ballet Studio, Miss Carmen Estrellada*. There is a painting on the window of the door in gold paint, the silhouette of a ballerina in fifth position.

We climb the stairs heading to the studio. The carpet is mushy and wet, and water still drips in spots from the ceiling.

"We probably shouldn't be here," says Nell, "but I wanted you to see."

As we go up the stairs, I don't hear the piano playing. I don't hear the dancers leaping on the floor. I don't hear Miss Estrellada's voice calling out steps. I only hear water dripping.

Sometimes the roof leaks in the summer at our house, when it rains very hard, especially upstairs in Wallace's old nursery. And sometimes it leaks in the ballroom, and we have to put a pan or a bowl under the leak. As the water drips in, it goes *ping-pong, ping-pong.* The sound changes as the water in the pan deepens. There are many different sounds of water dripping here, as we get to the top of the stairs, and I don't think a bowl or pan will fix things.

The glass door into the studio is locked, with a two-by-four nailed across it and a sign that says *Danger: Do Not Enter.* Through the glass, we can see that the ceiling has collapsed onto the floor. Plaster and big pieces of the ceiling have smashed against the dance barres and lie all over everything. There are big pools of water everywhere, and wet insulation hangs from the ceiling, dripping more brown water.

"Gee, what a big mess!" says Wallace.

"It looks like the Monster from Mars marched around in there," says Kip. "You know, those movies my dad watches late at night that show this big monster picking up the Empire State Building and with one gulp swallowing it whole." Kip starts acting the part of the monster, gulping and gnashing his teeth.

I don't say anything at all. I just think how different everything is now. I remember just a week ago, climbing these stairs with Nell, hoping to get a chance to try out for the recital. I remember the happy feeling I had, hearing the piano pouring out the notes I loved to hear. Now all the joy of the dance studio is smashed with the smashed ceiling and the brown water dripping. I look at Nell, whose face is desolate, pushed close to the glass door, with her ballerina's hands wrapped around the two-by-four and the big, ugly danger sign.

I think of the Cuban government dragging Miss Estrellada's piano out of her tiny apartment, the soldiers circling the piano like a trapped animal. I think of her fiancé lying in the road near a palm tree that shudders in the wind. I think of Miss Estrellada's pupils at the barre working hard, my friend Nell among them, Nell who has been so good to me.

Then I think of the kids at school, and how they'll probably hate me when everyone figures out where Wallace and I live. Then they'll know the terrible thing that happened to us there. They'll swarm up here again and stare, the way they did before. Wallace and I will be outcasts and no one will understand. But Nell didn't hate me when she found out where I lived.

I think, too, of the auction we had, that dreadful auction, when all the antique dealers came to buy all our furniture, all our possessions. Many of them came just out of curiosity. How curious the people in town have been since the "incident."

Then I think about Nell again and how hard she's worked and all the things she has taught me. I think of all those mornings we worked together in the gym. Then it occurs to me that maybe her hard work would not be lost forever if the recital could still take place, and even if I wasn't a part, I would be a host. I would be hosting the recital and in some ways that was better than no recital at all.

"Okay," I say, "you can ask Miss Estrellada if she wants to have the recital at my house. I know my mother won't mind."

Nell leaps up and does a tour jeté. Kip and Wallace cheer, "Yeah! Hurrah! Yeah! Hurrah!" And I stand there, not saying anything at all.

"Let's go tell Miss Estrellada about my idea now," says Nell. "Come on. I'll take you to her house. Let's go."

Outside on the sidewalk, Nell and Kip and Wallace pull and push me along the ice the whole way there, but I hold back, like a sled with a broken runner.

CHAPTER XVII

In Miss Estrellada's house, everything is white — a white sofa (not a couch and not a davenport), a white woven rug in the middle of the room turned on an angle, two white butterfly chairs in wrought iron with white canvas slings fitted over them to sit on, white walls and white linen curtains draped at the windows.

"Little Nell, come in," says Miss Estrellada. "I've been crying for our studio, Nell. Come in, and we'll cry together, both of us," she laughs.

We troop in behind Nell, and Miss Estrellada says, "You've brought your friends, I see."

And Nell says, "Yes, this is Kip. He's probably going to Schenectady, New York, for a whole weekend."

"Hello," says Miss Estrellada.

"And this is Wallace. She ran away last night."

"Oh, this is the little girl who ran away!" says Miss Estrellada. "You gave the whole town a terrible scare."

Wallace looks down at her feet and doesn't say hello.

"And this is Fiona, my friend who wants to be a ballerina."

"A lovely thing to wish to be. You should come to my school, if I ever have a school again," she says, sort of laughing. "Would all of you like a cookie?"

Miss Estrellada goes off into her small kitchen, which is through two little swinging-shutter doors. From here, I can see only her feet on a green-and-black marble patterned linoleum floor.

"I guess a lot of electrical power is off, and phone lines are down, but as you can see, my lights are working," she calls from the kitchen.

On the wall in the hallway is a photograph taken of Miss Estrellada in Cuba after a ballet performance. She is receiving a huge bouquet of white flowers.

"That was after I danced Giselle in Cuba," she says, coming into the living room with a plate of gingerbread dancers. "Calla lilies were my favorite flowers. Those flowers were from my fiancé, who was the young conductor of the orchestra that played the beautiful music. Here are the cookies. I made these for my classes to eat this week as a treat for everyone's hard work, but now we will not be having class till who knows when."

Kip takes two cookies, one for each hand, and so does Wallace. In fact, Wallace puts a third one in a pocket, and I nudge her with my elbow.

Wallace says, "Quit it, Fiona."

I only take one cookie, and then I don't eat it. I just sit down on one of the butterfly chairs and hold the cookie on my lap. Wallace is getting crumbs all over Miss Estrellada's white rug, and she has cookie crumbs all over her cheeks.

"Wallace," I say, pointing to her cheeks and then to the floor. And Wallace whispers, "Shut up."

"You see," says Miss Estrellada, "Cuba is so very different from upper New York State and this little town. We don't have snow at all in Cuba. We have tall palm trees that rattle and dance their leaves at you as you walk by. They wave and say, 'Have a nice day! Be happy!' There are sugarcane fields and long roads lined with palm trees and great tall ferns with pointy shadows that say, 'Be happy. Dance! Dance!' "

It seems as if Miss Estrellada is telling us a little story. She waves her arms around and bends at the waist to mimic the palm trees. Wallace's eyes look as big as two pancakes, the great, huge ones Kip makes when he comes over on Saturday morning. (The ones that are so huge, one pancake fills a whole pan.)

"That's what the palm trees and the shadows on the sandy road said to me. They said, 'Dance like the wind, Carmen,' " says Miss Estrellada, and then she says it in Spanish. The sounds roll off her tongue and remind me of a birdsong.

"Before the revolution, I lived with my parents in a great, big, white house made of what you call stucco, I think," Miss Estrellada says, and waves her arms to show the size of the house. "There was a large courtyard in the middle of this house and at night you could sit out there and listen to the palm trees, going this way and going that way in the wind. That's my Cuba, Nell. That's how I remember it. So you see how all this ice and snow has baffled me. I wake up in the morning and I look out my bedroom window and I think, *What is all this crazy white stuff?*"

"It's snow," says Wallace, laughing. As she laughs, she spills more cookie crumbs on her coat.

"I've been to Seattle, Washington," says Kip, "and they hardly ever see any snow there. My uncle drives a truck in a forest of hanging moss. He's a park ranger and he wears a uniform."

"It doesn't snow in Seattle?" asks Miss Estrellada.

"Not much, but it rains all the time, and there's tons of mist everywhere," says Kip.

"And beards of moss," says Wallace, "that hang down all over the place, and people live under the beards."

"No, they don't," says Kip.

"Yes, they do," says Wallace. "My teacher told me. I want to live under a beard of moss," says Wallace, "when I grow up."

"It doesn't snow in California or Florida," I say, remembering the weather map at school and Miss Johnson drawing an arrow across the map showing the jet stream.

"Perhaps I should move to California, where there is no snow," says Miss Estrellada. "But then what would I do with my little dancers?" Miss Estrellada looks out the window and says to no one in particular, "And besides, I have a dance studio that needs repairs."

"About the recital . . . ," says Nell, very slowly. "If we found a new place to hold it, could we still have our Christmas dance recital?"

"Well, I suppose we could," says Miss Estrellada. "Have you thought of something, Nell?"

And Nell says, "Miss Estrellada, we have the *perfect* place. It's at her house." And she points to me. "She has a dance hall. I mean, a ballroom with a stage at one end. It's perfect."

"Where is this place?" says Miss Estrellada.

"Just outside of town on the big hill overlooking the river," says Kip. "It's near a real Indian burial ground. Once I found a piece of an Algonquin Indian necklace there."

"I found that, Kip," says Wallace.

"You threw it down, Wallace, and said you didn't like it, so I picked it up," says Kip.

"But I found it first," says Wallace.

"How big is the room?" asks Miss Estrellada.

"Oh, huge," says Wallace, "with plenty of echo, so when we sing, it sounds great."

"We need to put in a woodstove, but there's a place for one in the chimney," I say quietly.

"My dad can do that. He's a plumber and a furnace doctor.

You can call him Dr. Jones. Dr. Jones to the rescue." Kip is starting to shout with excitement.

"We even have a piano," says Wallace, and then she throws herself into the white sofa. "It's kind of broken, but Fiona can play "O Holy Night" on it, even in the dark, boarded-up room where it is. She doesn't have to see. She can tell by hearing."

"The piano is on wheels," says Kip. "We could roll it out of there."

"It's out of tune," I say.

"The room is *perfect*," says Nell. "I saw it. I knew the minute I saw it."

Then the telephone rings, and Miss Estrellada goes off into the kitchen and leaves all of us sitting there in her white, clean living room. Finally I decide to eat the cookie, and it tastes gingery and sweet, and I lay my head back in the butterfly chair and dream for a moment that I am dancing the part of Giselle, amidst all these beautiful, white flowers that are falling all around me.

Chapter XVIII

Miss Carmen Estrellada pulls up in our front yard in her green Studebaker. Wallace runs through the house yelling, "She's here! She's here again!"

This time Miss Estrellada's carrying a box of decorations for the stage. Sparkling ribbons and silk sashes spew out of the top of the box and trail behind her in the snow. She's bringing things in for the Christmas recital we are going to be hosting here at our house — the Wallace Hotel, as Kip calls it.

"Miss Carmen Estrellada is here!" calls Wallace at the top of her lungs. She runs over to the door, jumping up and down, and then when Miss Estrellada steps into the house, Wallace goes all quiet, tucks her head down, and stands there with one foot on top of the other.

Miss Estrellada carries the box up to the ballroom, sequins and shiny, silver stars falling on the steps behind her. Then she comes back down, brushing off her hands. Wallace and I are still standing in the hallway when she comes back through, smiling and moving across the floor as if she were balancing a book on the top of her head. She sweeps back out to her car for another box.

"Miss Carmen Estrellada is a prima ballerina, Wallace," I say. "She's from Cuba. She defected."

"Did she go to the doctor?" Wallace says, opening her eyes wide like our Betsy Wetsy doll, whose eyes won't close anymore. They're just stuck open, no matter how many times you tap her head.

"Wallace, *defected,* not *infected. Defected* means she left Cuba for good and she can't go back."

"Infected . . . defected . . . what's the big deal?" says Wallace, marching away and looking out the window at Miss Carmen Estrellada, who's closing up her car and carrying a huge cardboard moon across the yard.

"Wallace, go help her," I say.

"No," says Wallace, "she doesn't want any help."

"Go help her, Wallace," I say again.

"I can't," says Wallace. "I just can't."

Wallace and I just stand there as if our feet were stuck to the ground, like we were caught in the Molasses Swamp in a Candy Land game.

Miss Carmen Estrellada leans into the hallway and then all we can see is this huge cardboard moon coming through the door. Wallace and I go over slowly, and we each grab a side of it, and all three of us carry the moon carefully upstairs.

○ ○ ○ ○

Miss Carmen Estrellada is in our living area having tea with our mother. (She loves Earl Grey tea, too.) Wallace and I are supposed to be doing our homework.

I'm writing a short paragraph about Eleanor Roosevelt, about how she helped poor people and gave speeches even though she was shy. Wallace is writing a report on parakeets. Wallace's report starts out, "First you put the water in the dish."

"Wallace," I say, "why don't you start out with a better statement? Say, something like 'Parakeets are found in many homes along the eastern seaboard.'"

"No," says Wallace, "that doesn't have anything to do with how you take care of parakeets." She chews on the end of her pencil, and then she ends up drawing a picture of Mrs. Braverman holding a parakeet. Wallace has been drawing lots of pictures of Mrs. Braverman and her birds. She's pinned them all over her room and all over the dining room.

I'm leaning against the dining-room wall next to the door to our living area. Through the door I can hear the teacups clicking in there and the spoons rattling against the china. My mother and Miss Estrellada have been in there a long time. They are murmuring, and I can't hear the words they are saying, so it almost sounds like they are singing.

I think Miss Estrellada is telling my mother about her fiancé and how he died and how she ran to him. I hear drifting words like *devastating,* and in a little while I hear the word *heartbroken.*

Then I begin to hear my mother talk. I can't hear much of what she's saying because she's speaking in a low voice, but I can tell my mother is talking and talking. Then I hear Miss Estrellada responding in a slightly higher voice with her beautiful Spanish accent. If I press my head against the door, I can hear phrases now, like *learning to trust again* and *opening back up to the world.*

I'm just finishing up my report. Wallace left hers on the floor looking all crumpled and wrinkled. This is all hers says:

How to Take Care of Parakeets
First you put water in the water dish. You put
seed in another dish. Then you put clean
newspaper in the cage.
The end. By Wallace Hopper.

Wallace was looking for a way out of doing any more, so when Kip's father stopped over and asked if anyone wanted a ride to Ralph's Red and White Grocery Store, Wallace leaped on the opportunity.

My mother opened the library doors and said, "I'll get my

purse." She looked over at us as if she had recently woken up from a long nap. She was wearing her checked blue-and-white dress and had a look about her like a freshly swept room.

I watch the Furnace Doctor's van pull away now, its tires spinning a little in the snow. I look out toward the woods for Miss Estrellada. She went out for a walk to pick a winter bouquet, and she's been gone a long time.

I stand at the dining-room window, and then I turn and look around the room. There must be a hundred drawings that Wallace has done in here on the walls, all of Mrs. Braverman and her parrots and warblers and finches. She drew them all in the last couple of weeks. There are also a couple of drawings of our father. Wallace gave him brown, sad eyes that seem to follow you around the room.

I'm just walking around looking at all the drawings, like I'm in a museum or something, when outside a car pulls up in the yard and parks next to Miss Estrellada's Studebaker. It's Nell's car, and Mr. Stamford is driving. He gets out and opens the trunk and starts lifting folding chairs out of the back. Then the side door pops open and Nell and three other kids from ballet class climb out of the car.

I slip into the hall and hide behind one of my mother's statues just as everyone comes in the front door. I pull back against the wall, but Nell sees me and hurries over to me and takes my hand.

"Oh, Fiona we've got some of the costumes today, and they are so beautiful!" she says.

In our hallway with its enormous ceiling, Alison Elkhart doesn't look as tall as she usually does. Alison rolls her eyes up and down and around, looking at everything. She says, "Neat place. Geez, who lives here?"

And Nell says, "Oh, Fiona and Wallace do." Then she pulls me up the stairs and says, "Come on. Come and see the costumes."

"Oh, I'll be up later. I have to get some lunch first," I say, looking out the window at the pair of marble swans sitting along the walk up to the porch outside. The snow and wind swirl around them.

Nell lets go of my hand and leaps up to the landing. "It's up here, everybody. You won't believe how great the stage is." Halfway up the stairs someone drops a little suitcase, and it pops open. Pink ballet shoes and red ribbon and fluffy tutus of pink netting scatter and spill all over the hallway floor.

I'm still leaning behind my mother's statue when Mr. Stamford comes through carrying several chairs.

"Hello there," he says. "Pretty big place you've got here. And it's perfect for the recital. Perfect!" He smiles at me as he carries the chairs up the stairs. "Aren't you coming up?" he says.

He doesn't seem to remember, or doesn't care, how I lied to him about our house that night in the rain. I follow him slowly, but when I get to the top step, I slip past the ballroom and go the opposite way down a hall toward my old bedroom.

When I open the large door, I can remember how the room once looked, and for a moment I'm surprised at how empty it is. In the summer I come up here to read, so there are bunches of books lying around on the floor. There's *The Child of Snow* with its beautiful cover, a picture of a little girl wrapped in a pale-blue scarf and coat, heading out into a white-on-white snow-storm, carrying a glowing candle.

There are other books, too. *The Railway Children, The Yearling, Little Women,* all of them exactly where I put them, exactly where I lay and read them on long, undisturbed, quiet afternoons last summer. Maybe this house isn't so bad after all. Everyone in the ballet class seems to love it.

I go over to my old bed. It's built right into the wall with a blue-painted, wooden front. I climb into it and sit in there. There's no mattress anymore, so it's like sitting on the floor. From here I can see the huge poplar trees in the yard below. In the summer, when the wind blows the silver leaves, it looks like thousands of dimes pouring through the branches.

I can see Miss Carmen Estrellada coming back from her walk. She is carrying a huge winter bouquet full of dried, brown flow-ers and stalks with orange berries on them and seed pods with curling backs. The brown-and-red-and-white bouquet towers above her as she walks along.

When I see Miss Estrellada smiling, carrying flowers that she found in the middle of winter, I think of the things she was saying to my mother, the words I heard . . . *trusting again* and *opening back up to the world*. I'm not completely sure what she meant, but those words keep floating through my head.

I get off my bed and sit down on the floor among my books, picking them up, remembering things.

After my father died, people from town swarmed up here. Reporters took pictures of the house. People tried to sneak around and look in the windows. These were people we didn't know, since we only lived up here in the summer. We didn't want anyone snooping around. We didn't want people to look at us. That's when we closed up all the windows in the big wing. My mother pulled heavy curtains across the windows, or tried to nail wooden shutters over them. We never wanted anyone to see our house. We thought if they saw our house they would know what happened here and they wouldn't like us anymore.

Once two women who live near us stopped by, carrying a covered dish. Maybe it was a chocolate cake. It could even have been a pineapple upside-down cake, my favorite, I don't know. But my mother wouldn't answer the door for a long time. When she finally did, she said we didn't like cake, that we never ate dessert. Then she slammed the door shut.

It turned out that when my father died he left a lot of bills. He'd had so many parties. We owned so many houses. He had spent more money than we had. We had to sell our winter house in Connecticut because we couldn't pay the taxes, and we had to have an auction here because we had no money.

At the auction, people from all over the place drove up in cars. They parked right on the flowers and grass in the front yard. The auctioneer set up a portable toilet right outside our living-room window. People swarmed all over the place carrying our things, a wooden chair of mine with a little bird painted on the seat, the desk my father always used in his study, the dining-room table that was so shiny you could look into it and see everyone sitting there upside down. I looked out the window and saw someone put Wallace's wooden dresser in their car.

My father had given me a book called *Dancing at Home*. It showed pictures of ballet steps and ballet techniques and it told how you could practice at home. During the auction I remembered I'd left it on the dining-room table. I hurried out to find it, squeezing through the crowds outside the library. I saw a man holding up a magnifying glass looking at a vase my grandmother had given us. I passed a woman crouching over a teapot trying to read the label on the bottom. My mother always kept that teapot in her studio. Sometimes she even put flowers in it.

When I got to the dining room, the table had already been sold. I finally found the book lying in the corner on the floor. I carried it back to the library and shut the door. Since then I have never let that book out of my sight, and up until recently I have never missed a day practicing. I pick the book up now. It has an inscription in the front. It says *For Fiona, my little ballerina, love from Daddy.*

I'm going to start practicing ballet again. I've decided just now. I'm *not* going to quit. Even though I didn't get to be in the recital this year, there's always next year. I'm going to keep practicing on my own, and I'm going to help paint the stage. And I'm going to help work on the set for the Christmas recital. And I'm going to practice and practice and practice.

CHAPTER XIX

Things are really different around here now. Nell is at my house almost as much as Kip is. She even brought Kenny here one day. That was the day Shorkey was visiting. Kenny and Shorkey spent the whole time sending Pez candies back and forth to each other in the dumbwaiter and climbing all over the swan statues that sit out in front of our house. When it was time to go home, we called Kip's father, and Kenny and Nell went home in the Furnace Doctor's van. When I leaned in the van to say good-bye, Nell was happily sitting on a toolbox and Kenny was lying down with his head on a length of furnace piping.

We've also been doing all kinds of work on the ballroom. It looks so much better. We've been painting and cleaning and freshening everything. One afternoon I went up to the ballroom to do some touch-ups on the trim around the doorway before Nell and Miss Estrellada and all the dancers got here.

I stopped before I went into the room, because my mother was up there, sitting over by the record player. I was surprised to see her, because she never seems to be interested in music anymore, even though it used to be one of her favorite things.

Now she was leaning down to put on a record. Then she just sat there listening to the jazz saxophone playing "I'll Be Seeing You." My mother had a peaceful expression on her face, a calm, accepting look. I stood there and listened and then I backed away and slipped downstairs and let my mother be.

In these last couple of weeks, Kip has thought of some more great sandwich names, and Nell even submitted one of her own. She wouldn't tell me what it was. I put in a few, too, but Kip's are by far the best. He thinks, night and day, of sandwich names. Sometimes we'll be walking along or having lunch or passing each other in the hall at school, and he'll tell me his latest sandwich name.

"How about a Succotash Submarine, an Indian-corn and bean mixture?" Kip whispered in my ear before he went in to the lunch line yesterday.

"A Huckleberry Hamburger," Kip called across the gym when we were having assembly.

"Not bad, Kip," I shouted back.

One night, I even received a phone call from Kip with a sandwich idea at about nine-thirty, just before we went to sleep!

Everything is changing around our house. Miss Estrellada has been here many, many times, getting things ready for the performance. It seems as if her Studebaker is always parked here in our front yard. I heard Miss Estrellada telling my mother one day in the hallway, "Thank you for having me and my dancers. I feel at home here. This house reminds me of the house I grew up in in Cuba, before the soldiers came one day and said to us, 'This house is no longer yours.'"

My mother has been working a little in her studio on the statue of Wallace, and she has been helping more and more every day with the props. She offered to sew up costumes that needed adjustments. She offered to help put together the silk flowers for the dancers to wear in their hair.

Just as I'd promised myself, I started to practice ballet again in the early morning. Kip's father and Kip brought over a big pot-bellied stove that had been in their garage. It fit in the chimney in the ballroom just right, so I had a woodstove to warm the room as I practiced. Before I went to work, I would run out to the woodpile and bring in an armload of wood. Then I'd put the music on.

A week ago, I was showing Nell my dance routine with the record "Blue Moon" playing. I had my toe shoes on, and I ran through the whole thing while Nell sat on a wooden crate on the floor, watching and listening.

Blue moon, you saw me standing alone, without a dream in my heart, without a love of my own. I went through the whole dance without a mistake. I imagined as I danced that I was onstage in England with the Royal Ballet, doing a pas de deux with Rudolf Nureyev. As I danced, I felt I must be flying. *Blue moon, you saw me standing alone, without a dream in my heart, without a love of my own* . . . fifth position . . . balancé . . . balancé . . . *Blue moon, you knew just what I was there for, you heard me saying a prayer for* . . . pirouette . . . jeté . . . arabesque . . . third position . . .

Halfway through the dance I looked at the end of the ballroom, and standing by the door was Miss Carmen Estrellada. She was standing stock-still, holding a large armload of fluffy, white tutus that from this distance could have been flowers in her arms.

I didn't want to stop the dance until the end, so I finished. I just kept on dancing. *Blue moon, you saw me standing alone, without a dream in my heart, without a love of my own.*

When the record was over, I stopped short and stood there staring at Nell and Miss Estrellada.

Miss Estrellada was like a statue, motionless. It seemed I stood there forever, while Miss Estrellada remained frozen, like the marble angel in the snow outside. Finally she began to move, and she said, "Tell me, little girl, how, how did you *ever* learn to dance like that?" Her voice with its accent echoed in the ballroom.

Then she said, "Nell, you didn't tell me your little friend could dance like that. You didn't tell me that *this* little girl, *this* little girl," she repeated very loudly, "*this little girl can really, really dance!*"

Miss Carmen Estrellada put her hands over her face for a moment. Then she looked up at Nell again and said, "Nell, is this the little girl who you told me you were teaching ballet to?"

And Nell said, "Yes, Miss Estrellada."

"Is this the little girl who you taught all the steps to?"

And Nell said, "Yes, Miss Estrellada."

"This is the child who knows the recital by heart?" said Miss Carmen Estrellada. "*This* is the girl?"

And Nell said, "Yes, Miss Estrellada. Yes, yes, yes."

And then Miss Carmen Estrellada said, "Nell, this girl is one of the best little dancers I've ever seen. This little girl is a soloist, Nell. That's what she is."

Miss Carmen Estrellada started walking back and forth in front of the stage, rubbing her forehead. "We will make a part for her in the Christmas recital," said Miss Estrellada to Nell. "She will play the part of the full moon. She will be the personification of the full moon that beckons the flowers to bloom in the snow for just one hour. You will dance the part of the moon," she said to me. "We will dress you in blue, and you will be the blue moon, like your song."

Nell shrieked at the top of her lungs, "FIONA, WE DID IT!

WE DID IT, FIONA. WE DID IT. WE DID IT." Then she hurled herself across the stage and threw herself into my arms.

"Nell," I screamed, "Nell, what did Miss Estrellada say? What did she say? Did I hear it right?"

"You're going to be in the Christmas recital, Fiona," said Nell.

"What did she say, Nell? What did she say?"

"You're going to be in the Christmas recital. We did it, Fiona. WE DID IT," Nell said, and then we both started to cry. For me it was like a dam broke; I just stood there, and I cried and cried and cried.

It turned out that the piano in the back room off the ballroom wasn't all that bad. It was dusty and badly out of tune, but it was playable. Miss Estrellada had a friend of hers who tunes pianos come over and tune it. He used little hammers and laid his head on the piano as he listened for the pitch.

Kip filled the potbellied stove with wood, so the huge room was toasty and the windows steamed over with warmth. I swept the floor and scrubbed the stage with a scrub brush and sponge.

We hung up garlands of evergreen that my mother wove out of boughs of pine from the woods around our house. My mother was working away down in our living area, and every so often she came upstairs with another draping garland. We hung them across the stage and all down the stair banisters.

Kip's father and our mother went out into the woods and found a very tall Christmas tree for the ballroom and stood it up in a bucket of water weighed down with rocks. Wallace and Nell and I decorated the tree with tiny, gold stars we made with glitter and papier mâché.

Everyone brought chairs. Nell's father drove up in his Pontiac and unloaded ten folding chairs that came from the Knights of Columbus hall. Kip brought another eight chairs from the kitchen set in his trailer, and Miss Estrellada had already brought about twenty folding wooden ones from her studio.

Soon the whole ballroom was full of chairs and garlands and wreaths and the tallest Christmas tree I've ever seen. The piano was tuned and polished and sitting off to the side. Kip helped construct a curtained-off area for backstage, to use for costumes and makeup.

The programs were run off on a mimeograph machine, and Wallace drew a big, blue moon on each one, with four or five flowers blooming in the moonlight. She worked away one whole afternoon on the drawings for the program, sprawled out on the floor up on the stage.

When my mother walked through the dining room one afternoon, she paused and looked at all of Wallace's drawings of Mrs. Braverman. Kip and Nell and I were sitting up on the sideboard taking a break, swinging our legs back and forth and eating M&Ms.

"What do you know?" our mother said to us, shaking her head and putting her hands on her hips, "Through all of this, through all of this, it looks like Wallace may have actually become an artist."

Kip did a lot of carpentry work upstairs. He hammered loose floorboards and fixed missing spindles on the stair banisters. Once in a while, he got carried away and started hammering on all the chairs and running around pretending to hammer people's heads. Then he did a hammerhead shark routine, which involved chasing Nell and Alison around the piano about ten times. But then he settled back down to work, helping adjust the lights so they shone on the big, cardboard, fluorescent moon and on the fluorescent stars painted on the black cloth of night that hung along the back wall of the stage.

As I went through rehearsals and I learned my part, written in for me by Miss Estrellada, the part of the full moon waking the flowers, I thought, *Oh, I must be flying.*

On the night of the performance, three days before Christmas, everything was set and perfect. The stage glowed. The Christmas tree was decorated. The lights were adjusted.

Many people from town heard about "The Dance of the Winter Moon," to be put on by Miss Carmen Estrellada's dance class. They heard, too, about the water damage and the ceiling collapsing at the studio. They wanted to come to the dance, and they also wanted to contribute a dollar to the studio repairs fund.

The people who came to see the dance were not just families of the dancers. There were others, too — the owners of Simon's Bakery, teachers from school (Miss Johnson and our principal), Marty Pippin from the newspaper-and-candy store, and Officer Wolf McKane. Even Mr. Braverman was there. He looked older and sadder now. Wallace hung his coat in the hallway, brought him a cup of cider and two candy canes, and sat with him in the front row during the performance.

There were some people I did not recognize at all. They were the ones who were curious about the old estate up here, but I felt ready, now, for them to see it. They hadn't been up here or seen the house in years, since my father died.

The night of the performance was a very special night for me. Lots of cars pulled up in our driveway and parked. We lit up the whole house. We went into the curtained and boarded-up rooms and pulled the shutters or curtains away from the windows and lit up every single room. The house was ablaze with lights, and there were candles in all of the many, many windows.

I thought a lot that night about Franklin and Eleanor Roosevelt, and how they had that terrible thing happen to them, when President Roosevelt got polio, and yet they were able to go on and do great things. Not just good things, but *great* things.

When our house was full of all the people who came to see "The Dance of the Winter Moon," the man from Simon's Bakery stood up.

"I'd like to make a short announcement," he said. "We have a winner for the 'Name That Sandwich' contest, and the winner is Wallace Hopper, for her sandwich, the Wallace Whammer. This sandwich is made with ham and melted cheese and olives and pecans. Wallace Hopper will be taking her family to the Biltmore Hotel in Schenectady, New York."

The crowd cheered; that is, everyone except for Kip. He looked heartbroken, like his face was a puzzle and all the pieces had been knocked out onto the floor.

"Don't worry, Kip," Wallace shouted. "You're *part* of my family."

Then Kip started smiling, and soon he was cheering, too.

When the lights began blinking, everyone settled down. (Shorkey was running the lights and Kenny was his helper.) Then the lights went off in the ballroom. The spotlight shone on the curtained stage, and Miss Estrellada and the boy with the violin began to play softly, the violin notes trembling and wailing just like a voice singing.

Then the curtain opened and I was the first to be seen, dancing the part of the moon in a blue, gauzy, net costume, waking up the flowers, calling them out of the frozen ground. I danced around Nell, the white Camellia Princess, and I danced around the Rose Petal Princess and the Lilac Princess and the Pansy Princess, and they came to life as the snow sifted down, and as they woke up and came to life, they danced.

As I was dancing, I looked out and saw Kip sitting there in the front row in his sport jacket and necktie, and I thought he looked very handsome. Then I looked two rows back and saw that Kip's father was sitting with my mother, and she was smiling. Her head was tilted toward him, and it wasn't a faint, distant smile, like she usually has. It was a full, real smile.

I danced then as I have never danced before. I danced that night for my daddy. In some ways I said good-bye then to my sadness, and I let it go like a flower floating off through the snow. I danced and danced and danced, and as I danced I had tears in my eyes, and I thought, *Oh, I must be flying.*

So that's how it was in our little town whose name means "little place where the wind stirs" in Algonquin Indian, and that's how it was on that once-in-a-blue-moon night at the Wallace Hotel.